FAKETASTIC

FAKETASTIC

a **FRENEMIES** *novel*

ALEXA YOUNG

HARPER TEEN

An Imprint of HarperCollins Publishers

HarperTeen is an imprint of HarperCollins Publishers.

Produced by Alloy Entertainment
151 West 26th Street, New York, NY 10001

Library of Congress catalog card number: 2008928091

ISBN 978-0-06-117570-1

Design by Andrea C. Uva

❖

First Edition

For Mom and Dad,
who always keep it real

The Style Snarks

DON'T GET DRESSED WITHOUT US!

Party Fouls!

posted by avalon: tuesday, september 30, at 7:07 a.m.

If you were at the social event of the season on Saturday (thrown by yours truly), you probably already witnessed some of the public displays of *affliction* exhibited by a few of the questionably clad guests. But just in case you missed them (like that's possible), here's a quick rundown of the biggest NOs of the night:

1. **Heather "Pleather" Russell.** Sorry, Heddy, but you've been found guilty of raiding the Pussycat Dolls' closet. That shiny, tiny hiney-band belonged on your head, not your hips.

2. **Jenny "Fur-Ball" Morgan.** Please tell us that fuzzy collar was faux and you didn't actually do something desperate to the cute little chinchilla you brought in for show-and-tell at Muir Elementary. Either way, at least you'd have an alibi for the red marks you've been sporting on your neck ever since. We'd buy it. (The excuse, not the fur!)

3. **Tyla "Tutu Tutu Much" Walker.** Nice effort, sweetness, but we were hosting a fashion-themed fete, not auditions for *Swan Lake.*

Better luck next time, girls.

Word to your closet,   Shop on,
Halley Brandon   *Avalon Greene*

PS: Yes, the rumors are true: No matter what went down between us at the party, Halvalon is back and better than ever. YAY! ☺

PPS: Big props to you for finding the new home of Seaview Middle School's most worshipped column ever—where disqualification from the *Daily* competition for being überfierce obviously just made us hotter (and fiercer)!

COMMENTS (59)

Yippee! I knew you wouldn't stay broken up 4ever. This blog RULES! (And great party, btw. Did U like my dress??? Please say YES!)
posted by realitease on 9/30 at 7:23 a.m.

OMG. Seriously? I would never forgive someone who outed my crush. Halley, U R way 2 nice. I'll B waiting 4 U 2 kick Avalon back 2 the curb. Go, Team Halley!
posted by tuffprincess on 9/30 at 7:26 a.m.

Got 2 agree with tuffprincess. I'm not sure I believe you 2 made up, anyway. I mean, what Avalon did was totally un4givable.

posted by madameprez **on 9/30 at 7:29 a.m.**

Fierce-o-rama! The only thing hotter than this column was that crazy video of Avalon's gymnastics performance. Cannot believe how her boobs were jiggling to the Dead Romeos song. HILARIOUS! Glad to see U can laugh it off, Av. That's so, um, BIG of you. xoxoxo

posted by superstyleme **on 9/30 at 7:34 a.m.**

Well, I liked Tyla's tutu! But good call on the pleather and the fur-ball. (And FYI, Jenny's neck was courtesy of Jordan Campbell. The dude is a total vampiromaniac neck-mauler. Seriously. BTDT! ☺)

posted by luv2gossip **on 9/30 at 7:46 a.m.**

This blog sucks. For real reporting, check out the actual WINNERS of the *Daily* competition: Margie and Olive. Click here for their stupendous Disease of the Day column!

posted by dissect_this **on 9/30 at 7:59 a.m.**

BFFs are the new black

"Isn't it amazing?" Avalon Greene breezed up behind Halley Brandon and gave her best friend's shoulders an affectionate squeeze.

The girls' golden retriever mix, Pucci—named after their moms' favorite designer—followed Avalon into the room and leapt onto Halley's boho-fabulous bedspread, where she began slobbering all over her new Chewy Vuiton squeak-purse.

"Amazing times infinity!" Halley's clear blue eyes sparkled as she swiveled her white egg-shaped desk chair away from their brand-new Style Snarks home page and grinned up at Avalon. Their first post since breaking free from Seaview Middle School's cyberzine, the *SMS.com Daily*, shimmered gold and pink from the screen of Halley's iMac.

"Take *that*, Miss Frey!" Avalon scoffed, grabbing Halley's hands and pulling her up from her chair.

"And *that*, *Daily*-dot-lame competition!" Halley giggled.

The girls bounced up and down as Madonna's "Material Girl" began playing through the computer speakers. Halley picked up the remote and cranked the volume as she and Avalon launched into a dance routine that predated Avalon's recent move from the gymnastics team to the cheerleading squad. Pucci barked and chased them around the room until a sound barrier–defying screech stopped the girls in mid-kick–ball change.

"OH. MY. *GOD!*" Halley's older brother, Tyler, squealed. The pale high school sophomore stood in Halley's doorway, clutching the sides of his face with his hands.

"Hey, Tyler," Halley said patiently. She tilted her head and smirked, totally unfazed by his glass-shattering volume. "What's up?"

"I thought we were having an earthquake!" Tyler bulged out his eyes and shook his head in mock horror so that his wavy dark hair flopped around his lightly freckled face. "But it was just Halvalon: The Reunion Tour." Tyler put his hand on his hip and contorted his face into an exaggerated perky smile.

"Uh, you think *that* was scary?" Avalon replied tersely, about to comment on Tyler's golfer-gone-wrong ensemble. But then she remembered how helpful Tyler had been with setting up the Style Snarks site the previous night and made an abrupt detour.

"What's really scary is how *hot* you look today. I almost didn't recognize you. That shirt is, like, full-on *adorkable!*" Avalon grinned. It wasn't a complete lie. The sky blue polo matched Tyler's eyes almost exactly and, combined with the faded green cargo shorts and white Chuck Taylor low-tops, did achieve a sort of geek-chic je ne sais quoi.

"This old thing?" Tyler locked eyes with Avalon, strutted toward Halley's bed, and then pivoted, supermodel style. "I was thinking of you when I threw it on, Avvy," he added in a breathy voice. *"Ciao!"* And with a flamboyant wave, he was gone.

"Dude." Halley giggled and shook her head. "Could my brother be more of a spaz?"

"Seriously." Avalon grimaced as she pushed a sheath of long, pale hair behind her shoulder. "You are so lucky it's not genetic."

"Yeah, except he's pretty awesome when he uses his supergeek powers for the greater good," Halley noted as she walked over to her desk and sat down at her computer. "I mean, dork or not, Ty definitely delivered last night."

"True." Avalon followed Halley to the desk so she could take a closer look at their shiny new blog for at least the hundredth time since they'd created it.

It really was beyond gorgeous. The idea for the website had come to Avalon in a moment of extreme inspiration right before bed. She'd immediately thrown on her pink Barefoot Dreams robe and cozy Ugg slippers, raced through the gate separating her family's backyard from Halley's, and gone straight up to her best friend's room. Minutes after gleefully telling Halley her concept, Avalon had registered the domain name and gotten down to business, with Tyler helping out on the technical end. But as much as Avalon and Tyler had contributed, it was the picture Halley had sketched of both girls looking adorably horrified as they tossed ugly outfits into Pucci's eager, drooling mouth that made the site spectacular. It was perfect. No, it was better than perfect. It was snarktacular.

"I am *so* in love with the logo!" Avalon clasped her hands to her heart excitedly. She was convinced Style Snarks would be the talk of Seaview Middle School, if not the entire town of La Jolla and city of San Diego. Maybe they'd even become international sensations, known for their ferocious-but-fair fashion assessments! "Thank *God* you took that graphic design course at art camp."

"I knew it would come in handy." Halley smiled at her best friend.

"You were right—for a change." Avalon giggled. "Seriously, this blog is already *so* much better than our competition column, isn't it?"

"Absolutely." Halley nodded reassuringly and twisted a lock of her long, wavy dark hair around an index finger. "This might just be your best idea *ever*."

Avalon wrinkled her nose and shivered with anticipation. It had been weeks since she'd felt this happy. But now it seemed all the awful things that had happened since Halley got back from art camp had just made Halvalon stronger than ever. The moment Avalon had seen Halley's mod-a-licious ensemble this morning—a white peasant top under a black velvet vest with skintight Seven jeans and haute-pink-patent wedges—she'd been convinced her best friend was really back this time. All the weirdness that had threatened to destroy eighth grade was so completely last weekend.

"Ooooh, comments!" Halley announced after she turned back to the iMac and refreshed the page.

A giddy smile played across Avalon's face as she leaned over Halley's shoulder to read the responses to their debut post. She was expecting the enthusiasm of the first com-menter to sweep across their readership. But with each word she read, she could feel more color draining from her face. The early feedback could not have been more anti-Avalon! A lump rose in her throat and she tried to cough it back down, just as Halley gasped audibly. They both laughed awkwardly to hide their simultaneous shock.

"Wow!" Avalon feigned delight while tugging at a lock of golden hair. "Looks like Team Halley found the site."

"What do you mean?" Halley turned and looked up, all wide-eyed innocence.

"What do you *think* I mean?" Avalon tried not to snap

at her best friend, but it was too late. She mashed her glossy lips together and then jumped onto Halley's bed to cuddle with Pucci. "You should *kick me to the curb* for outing your crush? The *hilarious* video of my gymnastics routine?"

"Dude." Halley rolled her eyes. "You had, like, fifty Avalon Teamsters cheering you on at school yesterday . . . *and* buying you lunch . . . *and* bringing you three different kinds of smoothies after cheer practice."

Avalon had to smile at that. Her supporters—led by pep squad captain Brianna Cho—had seriously rallied behind her. And Avalon couldn't help but feel sorry for her best friend when Team Halley's tragic attempt at support was blasting cheesy love songs in the middle of the quad. Halley must have been more embarrassed by hearing Christina Aguilera's "Beautiful" at lunch than she'd been by Avalon's impromptu performance of the song—slightly modified with Halley's crush-revealing lyrics—on Saturday night.

But now Avalon was worried. What if all their readers rallied around Halley? What if people thought Avalon was the villain, no matter how back on track she and Halley were? What if Team Avalon never found Style Snarks, or worse: What if they'd *disbanded*?

"Come on! Don't let it bum you out." Halley frowned emphatically. "This is exactly why creating our new blog is so important."

"Remind me of *exactly* why, again?" Avalon pouted as she rubbed Pucci's belly.

"Because now the whole school will see how recommitted we are to each other," Halley insisted, "and that we've united to save the school—one fashion disaster at a time!"

Avalon ran her fingers along Pucci's swirly orange and brown scarf, which complemented her own silky beige and tangerine–hued tank perfectly, and tilted her head in deep thought.

"Seriously!" Halley walked over to the bed to join Avalon and Pucci in a group hug. "Thanks to Style Snarks, *everyone* is going to be back on the same team: Team Halvalon for life! And it's all thanks to *you* for suggesting we start a blog."

Avalon finally returned her best friend's smile. Of course Halley was right. They'd always been unstoppable when they worked together. And now that they were reunited, nothing could get in the way of making eighth grade the best year of their lives.

Dazed and confused

The morning sun shone warmly on Halley's face as she breathed in the salty ocean air and lay back against the gray leather seat of Constance Greene's convertible BMW. Halley stole a glance over at Avalon, whose mind seemed to be as far away as the three hot-air balloons drifting above the Pacific coastline in the distance.

As Constance steered the car through the wrought-iron gates of SMS, Halley wondered if Avalon was still thinking about the harsh comments on their blog. She thought she'd convinced her best friend that everything would be fine, but she was eager to prove it to her.

"Ohmygod!" Avalon suddenly went from dejected to disgusted as the car came to a stop. "What is *that*?"

"Oooh, how fun!" Constance cooed sweetly, oblivious to her daughter's revulsion.

Halley looked toward the school's domed courtyard entrance, where two girls were performing some sort of ill-advised dance routine. One was about a foot taller than the other and both were wearing dark tights and knit hats and had attached black pillows to themselves. Bug eyes shot down from their crazy, thick-rimmed plastic glasses as the pair flailed around, holding signs that read: SAY NO TO GERMS! READ THE SMS.COM DAILY HEALTH COLUMN and YOU BE ILLIN'? DISCOVER THE DISEASE OF THE DAY AT SMS.COM DAILY.

"Do Margie and Olive really think anyone wants to read about snot and chicken pox?" Avalon frowned as she and Halley bade a quick adieu to Constance and kissed Pucci, who always rode shotgun, on top of her fuzzy strawberry-blond head. "Are they supposed to be germs? They look like insects!"

"Actually, I hear that cockroach couture is gonna be huge this year!" Halley giggled. "We should probably give them a style shout-out."

"Where's the bug spray when you need it?" Avalon said with a shameless snort.

Halley tried not to laugh as she watched a few students mimic Margie Herring and Olive Johnson. She almost felt sorry for them—*almost*. After the disastrous Halvalon disqualification from the school cyberzine competition, the rest of the student body had split their votes between the sports and music columns. So Margie and Olive's überserious health column had won by default.

But bizarrely tragic as this early morning spectacle was, it was also the unlikely inspiration Halley needed. "Hey, can I meet you in the cyberjournalism villa?" she asked Avalon as they headed through the Spanish-tiled lobby of the boutique hotel–turned–public school and arrived at their gold lockers.

"I guess . . . but why?" Avalon smirked. "Planning on stealing some Raid from the janitor's closet?"

"Maybe!" Halley tossed Avalon a sly grin. Margie's and Olive's costumes—and posters and slogans and, well, everything—might have been misguided, but advertising their column wasn't such a bad idea. Halley wanted to get a few supplies from the art room so she could design a killer ad campaign to drive traffic to the Style Snarks site—something sophisticated and cool that didn't involve dressing like parasites. Avalon would be *floored*. And thrilled. Hopefully.

"Whatevs." Avalon smiled back at Halley—until a mob of students with more faux tattoos and black eye makeup than a Fall Out Boy fan club stomped by. Avalon's grin faltered.

"Team Halley *RAWKS*!" two of the Pete Wentz wannabes shouted, nearly mowing Avalon down.

Halley's eyes widened in disbelief. Who *were* those people? She recognized a few from around campus, but she hadn't exactly hung out with—or even spoken to—any of them. Ever. Halley gave Avalon an *I have no clue* look, which apparently reassured her, because she quickly composed herself, turned on her Juicy Couture gladiator sandals, and chirped, "See you in a few."

Halley took several controlled yoga breaths as she walked to the art room, trying to put the Team Halley ambush behind her. The knots in her stomach had nearly come untied when, there in the middle of the hall, she saw Wade Houston. Lead singer of the Dead Romeos Wade Houston. Recently exposed supercrush Wade Houston. Walking directly toward her, Wade Houston.

Halley felt the knots return to her stomach . . . and shoulders . . . and neck. She wanted to duck behind something—*anything*—but there were just rows of lockers on either side of her. She had no choice but to meet Wade's mesmerizing gaze.

"Hey." He stopped less than a foot away from her and ran a hand through his messy black hair, which was starting to look less fauxhawked and more mop-topped.

"Oh, hey!" Halley felt queasier than she had after too many oysters on the half shell at Kylie Schwartz's bat mitzvah last year, but somehow managed to keep her voice as smooth as soy milk.

"Haven't seen you since your party," Wade said, his thick-lashed, dark brown eyes staring into Halley's.

Well, Wade, Halley thought, *that's because I've been avoiding you. I mean, I can't imagine you'd want to hang out with some dorktard who made up a song about how madly in love with you she is. Especially given that you're dating your guitarist, a.k.a. my good friend Sofee Hughes!*

"Oh yeah . . . I've been busy, I guess." Halley shrugged non-chalantly and tugged at the hem of her black velvet vest. At least her ensemble said, *You'd be* lucky *to date a girl like me.*

"Right." Wade squinted. Was it because of the sun streaming in through the skylight in the arched ceiling, or because he didn't believe her? Had he totally just read her thoughts? Was he as mortified as Halley that her crush on him had been announced so publicly? Was he *angry* about it? "Well, you got a minute to talk?"

Ohmygod. A mixture of fear, embarrassment, and panic threatened to paralyze her.

"Sure. Garden?" Painting on her most alluring Mona Lisa smile, Halley channeled all her energy into remaining calm. She spun around and led Wade out to the Garden of Serenity, one of her favorite spots on campus. Luckily, she thrived under pressure—on the outside, at least.

Just as Halley and Wade sat down on a stone bench under a weeping willow, two girls marched by in bright pink sweaters emblazoned with sparkly silver letters spelling the words TEAM AVALON.

"Your vid-e-o was su-per-lame. Av-a-lon will win this game!" bellowed the blond duo. The Avalon clones kept repeating their horrifying chant as they strode past the bench, over the koi pond bridge, and, finally, out of sight.

"Uh, friends of yours?" Wade grinned awkwardly, rubbing his palm against the faded brown cotton of his Carolina Liar T-shirt.

"Besties!" Halley said through gritted teeth, her right eye twitching slightly.

"Well . . ." Wade sighed and leaned back on the bench, biting his deliciously red lower lip in the most adorable way Halley had ever seen a lip bitten. "I actually kind of wanted to talk to you about, um, Avalon's song from Saturday."

"Oh yeah—wasn't that *awesome*?" Halley crossed and uncrossed her legs a couple times before she realized how obviously nervous it must look. She couldn't believe Wade was bringing up the song! Why couldn't he pretend it had never happened?

"Uh . . ." Wade shifted on the bench so that his right thigh collided with Halley's left one. She flinched at the physical contact and looked down, half expecting his hotness to have seared a hole in the dark denim of her jeans.

When she looked back up, Wade's eyes stared deeply into hers. Before Saturday, Halley might have interpreted such an intense gaze as Wade being interested in her. But now she knew better. Now it was clearly a look of pity. He was about to break up with her. And they'd never even dated! All of the horrible things he was about to say hit Halley like individual kicks in the face. He couldn't possibly hang out with a creepily obsessed freak. He didn't want her to be friends with Sofee, and he definitely didn't want her to help out with the Dead Romeos' publicity. Maybe he'd even threaten to get a restraining order.

"I don't know about awesome," Wade finally said. "But I haven't been able to get those lyrics out of my head. I mean . . ."

Ohmygod . . . ohmygod . . . ohmygod . . . Halley crossed her legs again and began jiggling her foot at warp speed. Her brain had turned to Jell-O, unable to control her body any longer.

This must be how stalkers feel when they get caught in celebrities' homes, she thought desperately.

"Well . . ." Wade paused. "The thing is . . . I kind of think I feel the same way about you."

WHAT? Halley uncrossed her legs, wiped her sweaty palms on her jeans, and then searched Wade's face for proof that he'd just said what she thought he'd said. There was no way. Halley tried to remember the exact words to her song: *"Yes, Wade, you're beautiful in every single way. So glad we finally found . . . all of the love we found today."*

Yikes. How tragic. Wait . . .

"Um, what do you mean . . . ?" Halley glanced over at Wade furtively.

"Well, I'm not gonna *sing* it." Wade broke into a broad, sheepish grin. "But, um, I like you too. A lot, actually. I have for a while."

Halley realized she'd been holding her breath and finally told herself to exhale . . . slowly. There was a fresh, cool dampness in the air as the birds began chirping in the weeping willow overhead, and the waterfall behind the bench shushed her into a state of Zen-like tranquillity. A few of her classmates glided by, turning to smile over at Halley and Wade. It was like they knew they were looking at the soon-to-be hottest couple at SMS. But then a far less soothing image invaded Halley's brain.

What about Wade's actual girlfriend? What about Sofee?

"So, uhhh . . ." Wade tilted his head, his beautiful face mere inches from Halley's—so close she could smell a hint of mint (wintergreen, perhaps?) on his breath. ". . . thoughts?"

"Well, um, hmmm," Halley stammered. "I mean. Yeah. I mean . . ."

Wade laughed through his nose in a way that said, *Halley Brandon, you're adorable.* "I'll take that as . . . maybe you want to hang out on Friday?"

Did he just ask me out? He did! He did! He did!

Halley wanted to savor this moment, but how could she when *What about Sofee?* was vying for the top thought in her head? All Halley could think about was Sofee finding her hiding in the limo after Avalon outed her crush in front of their entire party. How she had felt even more ridiculous when Sofee announced she and Wade were "kind of seeing each other."

"Um." Halley swallowed hard, trying to ask the question that would end this moment for sure, when the first-period warning bell rang. "Oh! Jeez! Can we talk later?"

"Totally." Wade nodded and grabbed Halley's arm to gently and oh so chivalrously help her up from the bench. "I'll call you."

Then he leaned in and gave Halley a quick good-bye peck on the cheek.

Oh. My. Freaking. God.

Halley was in a Wade-induced stupor as she raced through the main building. Just as she was approaching the art room, a tall, slender figure sped past a crowd of students and nearly slammed right into her. It was Sofee. Halley instantly snapped out of her Wade haze. She felt like she'd just been punched in the stomach.

"Hey, Sofee . . ." Halley said quickly. "What's up?"

"Oh, you know. The usual." Sofee straightened her back, holding her head a little higher than normal. She could not have looked more rockadelic: Purple highlights had replaced the blond streaks in her long, dark curls, and she was wearing a black tank dress over a gray long-sleeved thermal with plum-colored platform sandals that made her tan, slender legs look even longer than usual. "I've barely seen you since Saturday. How've you been?"

"Fine. Awesome!" Halley flashed a bright, exaggerated smile, praying Wade hadn't left some sort of brand on her cheek when he'd kissed her. Could Sofee smell the wintergreen? "How 'bout you?"

"Good," Sofee said flatly, then quickly added: "Oh . . . but

I guess I should tell you. Wade and I broke up last night. I mean, just so you know."

"Really?" Halley shuddered with a combination of excitement, sympathy, and uncertainty. "Wow. Are you—?"

"I don't really want to talk about it." Sofee cut Halley off with a stony determination in her dark eyes. "I'm over it."

Halley shuffled her pink wedges on the gold-carpeted hallway outside the art room. "Are you *sure*?"

"Yeah." Sofee bristled and shifted her gaze down to the ground. "I mean, I think so. Seriously, it's no biggie. What kind of girl lets some guy ruin her life, *right*?" Sofee looked back up, her face softening hopefully. Despite her attempted nonchalance, she seemed desperate for some sort of affirmation from Halley.

"Right. Of course. Totally." Halley grinned weakly and adjusted the multicolored L.A.M.B. Hella hobo bag on her shoulder.

"Anyway, I've gotta get to class," Sofee finally said, raising an eyebrow—the one with the tiny silver hoop in it. "I'll see you later, though?"

"Uh-huh." Halley nodded dizzily. She made her way into the art room, grabbed her supplies, and finally rushed back through the main building and out toward the journalism villa as a million thoughts raced through her head.

I need to talk to Avalon. She'll help me figure out what to do. But Avalon hates Sofee. Still, Avalon's the reason Wade knows I like him. So she's also the reason he likes me back.

But what just happened with Sofee? Could she really get over someone as amazing as Wade in just one night? Does she know Wade likes me? Was she just pretending to be nice? Should I have apologized to her? But I haven't done anything wrong. Have I . . . ?

The final bell rang, signaling the start of school.

Great, Halley thought. *I'm late for first period.*

If only all her problems were as simple as that one.

Merge with caution

Avalon walked through the dining hall toward the smoked-glass doors to the patio. The enticing aroma of the kitchen's California pesto pizza almost diverted her from her mission, but she kept moving. The only thing she was hungry for was information.

When she got outside, Avalon headed straight for her and Halley's usual table, clutching the *need to talk* note her best friend had passed her in cyberjournalism class. Should she be worried? Excited? Halley was already sitting at the glass-topped table with nothing but a bottle of Pellegrino. Apparently she wasn't in the mood to eat either. Was that a good sign or a bad one?

"Ohmygod, *what's* going on?" Avalon whispered loudly, sitting down in the green-cushioned patio chair next to Halley's.

"You'll *never* believe it." Halley bit her thumbnail and leaned in close.

"Try me." Avalon grabbed Halley's hand, always eager to save her best friend's manicure.

Halley drew in her breath and widened her pale blue eyes. Just as she parted her bubblegum-pink lips, a voice that was definitely *not* Halley's interjected.

"Avalon! Oh. My. Gosh!"

Avalon turned to see Brianna looking jittery and flushed, like she'd just downed a case of Red Bull. *As if.* The cheer captain would never resort to artificial pep. It was one of the billion things Avalon respected about her. Another was that she always seemed so in control. Until now.

"I've been looking all over for you!" Brianna gasped as she scurried up to the table.

Avalon was going to politely ask Brianna if she could talk to her later, but her friend was clearly on an überimportant mission, and besides, Avalon was too mesmerized by her ensemble to send her away. It was the most incredible gym-to-class coup in the history of multipurpose style: a red Stella McCartney for Adidas leotard under a pleated denim mini, with a killer red, gray, and dark purple striped scarf and matching leg warmers. On anyone else, it would have been a definite No. But on Brianna, it was a cheertastic Yes. It was *so Teen Vogue. So* daring. *So—*

Ohmygod, no way!

Avalon noticed the logo just above Brianna's right boob actually read ADIDOS. She was completely pulling off a fake.

Impressive!

"Bree! Love the leo." Avalon smiled.

"Oh! Thanks!" Brianna beamed, catching her breath. "Listen, can I talk to you about something? It's major. Like, the biggest news ever."

"Totally." Avalon ran her bronze-hued nails through her long blond hair and tilted her head inquisitively, trying not to seem too eager. But between whatever Halley had to tell her and Brianna's imminent announcement, she suddenly felt like the hottest reporter in town.

"In *private*," Brianna added, narrowing her almond-shaped eyes intensely.

"Oh, um . . ." Avalon draped her lightly tanned arm around the back of her best friend's chair. "We can talk in front of Halley."

"Really?" Brianna gave an uncharacteristic eye roll and sighed loudly. She sat down, pulled her chair closer to Avalon's, and glanced around furtively before acknowledging, "I guess this involves her too."

Avalon turned to give Halley a warm, reassuring smile, but quickly turned back to Brianna when she caught her best friend's irritated gaze. Brianna cleared her throat and leaned in so that her thick, silky black hair grazed the top of the lunch table. Avalon heard Halley sit back in her chair and take a big swig of Pellegrino.

"We've been invited to participate in the Regional Middle School Cheerleading competition," Brianna said in a low, deliberate voice. "Also known as the RMSC! *But* we need to increase the squad to twenty members and it's only three weeks away. So we're gonna take a vote this afternoon to merge the cheerleading and gymnastics teams."

O! M! G! Second to the reemergence of Halvalon, this was the biggest news Avalon could imagine. Giving up gymnastics a few weeks ago—just before she and Halley had completely divided their lives—was one of the hardest decisions Avalon had ever made. But now, it was like the extracurricular gods had read their blog and decided to solidify their reunion. Not only did they have their Style Snarks site uniting them, they'd get to compete on the same team again!

"But we need everyone to vote in favor of the merger," Brianna added, tugging nervously at one end of her scarf.

Why was Brianna so worried? *Of course* everyone would vote for the merger. There was no way the gymnasts wouldn't jump—literally—at the chance to compete in such a prestigious event. Plus, having more gymnasts on the squad would make the cheerleaders that much stronger, so they'd be on board, too. This was a huge opportunity for the gymnasts, the cheerleaders, *and* the new-and-improved Halvalon. A win-win-win. A match made in cheernastics heaven!

"But what if the gymnasts don't *want* to be cheerleaders?" Halley scoffed before Avalon could voice her wholehearted support.

Huh? Was Halley seriously *rejecting* the idea? She'd barely even taken a moment to think about how awesome it might be.

"Well, why wouldn't they?" Brianna asked, flustered, turning to Avalon for backup.

"Yeah, Hal, why *wouldn't* they . . . ?" Avalon shot a firm but pleading look at her best friend.

"I don't know." Halley shrugged and leaned back farther in her chair, crossing her arms over her chest. "Do you really think we're *peppy* enough?"

"Ohmygod!" Avalon giggled and waved a hand to dismiss Halley's silliness. "Don't even worry, Bree. Just let me talk it through with Halley and I'm sure it'll all work out."

"Yay!" Brianna's face lit up with excitement and she leapt up from her chair, shaking the patio table as she rose. "I knew we could count on you, Avalon! I mean, the squad will be devastated if this doesn't happen, you know?"

"Totally." Avalon nodded.

Brianna turned to walk away, but then spun on her adorable black patent flats and stared at Halley with a glint in her eyes. "I just hope the gymnasts are up to the task," she said ominously. "Cheerleading *is* a whole different game."

Avalon felt the heat rise to her cheeks as Brianna left the

table. She hated the tension between her friends—even though it was kind of flattering, like they were fighting over her. But that wasn't what was *really* upsetting her. Brianna had just questioned the gymnasts' pep squad potential, but *Avalon* had been a gymnast up until a few weeks ago. Wasn't she the best thing that had ever happened to the team? Brianna had always seemed so grateful to have her around. Avalon blinked hard and shook the uncertainty from her head. She needed to focus on the positives, like Brianna always said.

"So, you *are* going to go along with this, *right?*" Avalon asked, keeping her smile half-sarcastic so Halléy wouldn't get defensive.

"Is that a question or an order?" Halley glowered as she leaned forward and began tapping her dark pink fingernails on the tabletop.

So much for that strategy.

"Well, I obviously can't tell you what to do"—Avalon transitioned to a pout—"but I can't believe you'd consider passing up the chance to upstage the cheerleaders with your tumbling skills on a regular basis."

"Ha." Halley smiled.

Finally.

"Come on!" Avalon implored. "Can't you picture the pep squad lifting us up on their shoulders, celebrating their MVPs at the regional competition—just like the gymnastics team used to do?"

"Well . . ." Halley's icy exterior was melting.

"And don't you see that cheerleading is totally the new gymnastics?" Avalon challenged Halley with her dark eyes.

"But don't *you* realize nobody on the gymnastics team is going to follow Brianna's lead?" Halley's lip curled bitterly. "I mean, between the leg warmers, the scarf, and that lee-faux-tard?"

"Actually . . ." Avalon raised a pale eyebrow, trying not to giggle at Halley's pun. ". . . I kind of thought she pulled it off."

"You *cannot* be serious!" Halley shook her head incredulously and polished off the rest of her Pellegrino.

"Totally serious." Avalon nodded. "In fact, that gives me an idea for a new blog post. Let's go!"

As Avalon dragged Halley along the brick path to the journalism villa, she came up with a dozen more reasons the pep squad–gymnastics team merger made complete sense. As she rattled off each one, Halley's resistance grew weaker and weaker. And by the time they'd finished posting their latest Style Snarks column, Halley was sold like half-price couture.

The Style Snarks

DON'T GET DRESSED WITHOUT US!

SPECIAL REPORT: The Real Deal

posted by halley: tuesday, september 30, at 12:47 p.m.

We've all seen them: *Cucci* clutches, *Tammy* Hilfiger tops, *plastic* Prada. Wannabe-wear is an unfortunate part of the fashion world, and the less savvy shoppers among us are frequently fooled by these designer impostors. However, we recently discovered that even some of the best dressers in school are sporting phony fashions. So it's time for *everyone* to get smart about what's real and what's faux. Here are our three simple rules for spotting a knockoff:

1. **Look at the logo.** Now look closer. Whoops! YSL is for Yves Saint Laurent (and may he RIP). . . . VSL is for Very Sad Loser (and may that also RIP). RL is for Ralph Lauren. . . . PL is for Pretty Lame. D&G is for Dolce & Gabbana. . . . B&G is for Bogus & Gross. Get the picture?

2. **Check out the threads.** Sometimes the logo's real (or at least spelled correctly), but that's when the legit part quits.

News flash: If it looks like plastic and smells like plastic, chances are it's—say it with us—*PLASTIC*, no matter what that "Genuine Leather" stamp claims. And please don't tell us we need to help you distinguish between polyester and cotton.

3. **Try it on.** If you've selected the correct size, true couture will fit you like a glove—and *never, ever* cause muffin-top. Like a true BFF, it hugs you in all the right places. If that's not the case, then hello? It's probably faux. And a major NO.

Now for the less tragic part: Even we can admit it's not always completely criminal to wear knockoffs—*if*, that is, you're a born leader who can work it like it's real. (We'll *totally* grant you glamnesty if you can make a fake look even better than the original.) And speaking of born leaders: Word on the street is the cheerleaders and gymnasts may be merging into one super-tumbling team for the Regional Middle School Cheerleading competition! Could this be SMS's ticket to the big leagues? With the right person in charge, we'd say it's a done deal. Go, Lions!

Word to your closet,   Shop on,
Halley Brandon   *Avalon Greene*

Cannot believe you just said it's okay to wear a fake. What has come OVER you people?

posted by hotterthanu **on 9/30 at 12:59 p.m.**

Hey! That's awesome about the cheerleaders and gymnasts . . . but does this mean one of YOU will be taking over as captain? You're both born leaders, after all. ☺ Sounds like Team Halley and Team Avalon really are back together. Good luck with that! ☺

posted by luv2gossip **on 9/30 at 1:08 p.m.**

This is why I make all my own klothes. That way everything I wear fits and is real kouture. Project Runway, here I kome! lol

posted by kre8ivekween **on 9/30 at 1:17 p.m.**

I agree with hotterthanU. It's NEVER okay to wear a fake. No born leader would be caught dead in a knockoff, and there's no way to make a fake look better than a real piece. U guys should know that. Oh, and PS: Some designer clothes don't fit right. We can't all have the bodies of supermodels, you know? Nice try, though.

posted by vogue_us_baby **on 9/30 at 1:38 p.m.**

Rock the vote

*H*alley stood at the end of a single-file line, clutching a tiny slip of paper in her hand, waiting to drop her vote in the ballot box. She searched the faces of each gymnast and cheerleader for signs of how they voted as they made their way back over to the bleachers. Not that she had much doubt as to how things would go.

"Go, Lions!" Tanya Williams looked directly at Halley and smiled, her brilliant white teeth shining in the afternoon sun as she marched by. Tanya was an amazing athlete *and* cheerleader. She'd been Halley's doubles partner on the tennis team when Avalon had been sidelined with an injury, and had such a killer serve that people often asked if she was related to those other famous tennis players named Williams. "Teammates again?"

Halley smiled back and widened her pale blue eyes

enthusiastically. Even though she was a little annoyed that her lunchtime announcement had been preempted by Brianna, of all people, she'd decided it was better to save her Wade news until she could have Avalon's full attention. Besides, being on the same team with Avalon—and Tanya—*was* kind of exciting. Gymnastics hadn't been the same without Avalon—and maybe they could turn cheerleading into a real sport after all.

"Welcome to the squad, girls." Andi Lynch giggled quietly as she made her way past a few of the gymnasts. As usual, the petite brunette cheerleader sprayed saliva with each *s* she spoke.

I'm going to be a cheerleader. I'm going to be a cheerleader. I'm going to be a . . . cheerleader?

Halley tried to wrap her head around the idea of waving pom-poms in unison as she breathed in the bittersweet smell of the recently fertilized football field. At first, she'd cringed at the thought of transforming herself into a pillar of pep and dealing with Avalon's overly perky new friends. But Avalon, daughter of two lawyers, was born to argue her case, and managed to obliterate every possible objection. Halley also realized this was her opportunity to prove just how committed she was to her BFF, especially since she hadn't had a free moment to work on her Style Snarks PR campaign.

"Done!" Liza Davis, one of the most promising new members of the gymnastics team, blinked affirmatively at

Halley as she pranced by in a pale pink workout tank, her thick brown hair pulled up into a high bun. Clearly, Halley's efforts to rally the gymnasts using Avalon's arguments had worked. Finally, it was Halley's turn to vote.

"Last but not least!" Coach Carlson beamed up at Halley from behind a little folding card table, her red cheeks glowing with perspiration in the midafternoon heat. Unlike Coach Howe, who seemed young and lithe enough to be on the gymnastics team herself, Coach Carlson looked *nothing* like an actual cheerleader. But she did have the personality.

Halley grinned at the two coaches, dropped her vote into the box, and turned to join the rest of the girls on the bleachers.

"This is so crazy," Kimberleigh Weintraub said as Halley sat down next to her yellow-haired teammate. Kimberleigh flared the nostrils of her upturned nose; it was her favorite facial expression, overused to the point that Halley and Avalon had secretly named her Piggleigh Swinetraub. "I can't believe we're about to become cheerleaders."

"Okay, everybody!" Coach Carlson called a few minutes later. She clutched the ballot box in her sausagelike fingers. A tuft of her hair began flopping around in the light afternoon breeze like a frizzy orange shark fin. "We have the results of the vote, so let's all settle down!"

Halley glanced across the bleachers at Avalon, excited

to share this moment with her. But her best friend was embroiled in a dramatic whisper-fest with a few of the other cheerleaders. Oh well. They could celebrate later.

"So!" Coach Howe chirped, looking even tinier than her five feet in her navy unitard and warm-up pants. "It's a land-slide! We had nineteen yeses and just one no, so—"

"Congratulations!" Coach Carlson shouted, looking like she might literally burst out of her red, white, and blue striped sweatshirt-vest. "You're all cheerleaders now!"

"Woo-hoo!" Brianna cheered, bouncing off the bleach-ers and joining the coaches on the sidelines with Sydney McDowell, the little blond co-captain, leaping enthusiasti-cally behind her. "Gather up, everybody, and we'll get this party started with the Crazy V!"

"All right, all right, all right! Awesome, awesome, awe-some!" Sydney did a few kicks and toe touches, followed by a wavelike thing with her arm as she lunged and thrust her hips forward. "Come on, girls!"

Avalon excitedly wrinkled her nose at her best friend before racing over to join Brianna, Sydney, and the rest of the cheerleaders. Halley was about to follow Avalon when she noticed the gymnasts exchanging tentative looks, slowly shuffling onto the field. Halley tried to make eye contact with Avalon again, but she was already wrapped up in a cheer, executing several exaggerated jumps and dance moves with the rest of the pep squad.

"What do we do now?" Kimberleigh whispered to Halley. "Isn't anyone going to show us the routine?"

"Good question," Halley whispered back.

The gymnasts gathered into a cluster of awkwardness and continued to watch the cheerleaders, who were clearly unaware of the fact that half their newly merged squad hadn't joined them.

"Um, so who's the captain here?" Kimberleigh finally yelled over the chants of, "Lions, Lions, hear us roar!"

Halley bit her lower lip to stop herself from smiling and gave Kimberleigh's hand a light squeeze.

"What?" Brianna suddenly stopped bouncing around, and the rest of the cheerleaders followed suit. The smile disappeared from her face and she nervously straightened one of the straps on her Adidas leotard.

"Brianna's captain," Sydney quipped, putting her hands on her hips and cocking her butt to the side. Between her tiny orange spray-tanned limbs and tight white tank top, she kind of looked like an Oompa-Loompa. "And *I'm* co-captain."

"Right. Sydney's my second in command—like a vice president. And *I'm* like the president," Brianna explained slowly.

Halley wondered if Kimberleigh's questions had flustered the captain or if she actually thought pep squad politics was too complicated for lowly gymnasts to comprehend.

"And, like our coach said, you're *all* cheerleaders now!" Brianna recaptured her smile and whipped her black pony-tail from side to side as she turned to look in either direction for support. All the cheerleaders nodded effusively—even Avalon.

"Like *our* coach said?" Kimberleigh muttered under her breath.

"Actually . . ." Coach Howe strutted lightly across the grass and over to Brianna, with Coach Carlson ambling along behind her. ". . . Coach Carlson and I were just chatting about this."

Coach Carlson nodded at Brianna and Sydney, an apologetic smile spreading across her round face. "Cheerleading is all about unity, and everyone here is equally important to this new squad, so every single one of you needs to feel comfortable."

Sydney widened her violet eyes incredulously, while Brianna just stared down at her bright white Nikes, as she kicked a patch of dying grass.

"We're on a really tight schedule here," Coach Carlson continued. She wiped her palms against her tight royal blue shorts. "So, Bree, you and Sydney will teach everyone the competition routine, and in a week, we'll all vote on official leadership. Sound good?"

Although Halley couldn't see Brianna's face, the rest of the cheerleaders looked stunned—especially Sydney and

Avalon. When Brianna finally looked up, her dark eyes were blazing and her voice was peptastically clear:

"Sounds great! Let's do this, girls!"

"So, do all cheerleading practices go that well?" Halley grimaced as she and Avalon walked off the football field together. Finally, she had her best friend to herself while Brianna and Sydney hung back to meet with the coaches. Brianna clearly had her work cut out for her. By the end of practice, she'd looked like she might willingly give up her position to the first volunteer.

"Ugh, no." Avalon sighed, tugging her flaxen hair free from its ponytail like she was in a Pantene commercial. How did her hair always look so perfect, even after she'd been sweating for an hour straight? "That was *beyond* awful."

"I blame the captain," Halley said quickly, raising her dark eyebrows at her best friend.

"What?" Avalon scowled back.

"Hello? Brianna completely forgot there were ten new squad members there until Piggleigh said something." Halley shook her head. "And even after that, you were the only one who seemed to realize we might need someone to, uh, *lead* us a little."

"Really?" Avalon frowned. "It seemed like she was trying. . . ."

"Trying and failing." Halley sniffed.

"*Hal-ley*," Avalon whined with a wounded look in her eyes.

Halley pressed her lips together and tilted her head apologetically at her best friend. She hadn't meant to be so harsh—not to Avalon, anyway. The whole cheerleading thing just made her feel like a foreign exchange student visiting the oppressive, totalitarian country of Pepland. A subject change was definitely in order—and fortunately, Halley still had something totally un-cheer-related to discuss. That was when she caught sight of the topic du jour himself: Wade, leaning against an oak tree near the sidelines of the soccer field, was staring straight at her.

Ohmygod! What is he doing out here?

Halley tried to run a few fingers through her sweaty, tangled ponytail and then glanced down at her equally soaked gray sports tank and grass-stained white shorts. She could not have looked worse. And she was coming from *cheer* practice. How totally *un*–rock 'n' roll. Halley stole another glance in Wade's direction. Was he smiling at her?

She tried to keep her gaze fixed on the brick path ahead, but she could feel Wade's eyes on her—begging her to look over. She was about to comply when another spectator caught her eye.

No way! What is Sofee *doing out here?*

Halley felt like she was in a three-way tug-of-war. She looked frantically over at Avalon, who was stomping along the path next to her, her brow furrowed in thought. Halley obviously couldn't get Avalon's practical, bullet-pointed

39

advice about Wade now—and she *clearly* couldn't go talk to him in front of his ex. That left only one option.

"Hey, there's Sofee!" Halley blurted. "I need to talk to her about our art homework. Meet me in the locker room?"

"But . . . wait!" Avalon called, but Halley had already sprinted away.

As she got closer to Sofee, Halley told herself she could just chat casually about watercolors and pretend she hadn't seen Wade at all.

"Hi!" Halley smiled when she reached Sofee near the SMS villas. "How's it going?"

"Not bad." Sofee smiled back, her purple-streaked hair blowing gently around her flawlessly bronzed face. "I thought I might find you out here."

"Yup." Halley scowled as she tugged on the sleeves of the hoodie tied around her waist. "I'm, um, a *cheerleader* now." She couldn't believe she'd just said the words out loud—especially to Sofee, the guitar goddess and coolest girl on campus.

"Seriously?" Sofee offered a look of distressed sympathy.

Halley half shook, half nodded her head and rolled her eyes. "Tragic, right?"

"Uhhh." Sofee's face clouded over, but she wasn't look-ing at Halley anymore. "What's *Wade* doing out there? He's, like, allergic to athletic fields."

Halley tried not to panic as she turned around.

"Dunno." She managed to shrug nonchalantly, as though it were the first time she'd seen him. "Maybe he wants to be a cheerleader too?"

"Ha!" Sofee laughed caustically and gave the tiny diamond stud in her nose a light twist. "You would know."

What . . . ? Was that an accusation? Does Sofee know he asked me out?

"I'm sure he'd just do it for the uniforms." Halley quickly recovered.

But Sofee didn't even crack a smile. "Ew! He's not seriously talking to *her*, is he?" she practically spat, her eyes still trained in the direction of the soccer field.

Halley spun back around to see Wade and Avalon standing together, laughing like old friends.

"That *is* weird." Now Halley was confused too.

"Typical guy." Sofee frowned, squaring her shoulders and agitatedly tapping one denim sandal on the path. "None of them can resist Boobzilla."

A laugh and a cough met in Halley's throat. She was about to tell Sofee how ridiculous that was—but caught herself as she saw sadness and anger flicker in her friend's dark eyes.

"But I can't believe Avalon would do that to you," Sofee continued bitterly.

"What do you mean?" Halley asked, genuinely mystified.

"Well, hello? The girl outed your crush on Wade, like,

three nights ago, and now she's openly flirting with him!" Sofee shook her head furiously. "I mean, aren't you guys supposed to be friends again?"

"Yeah, but . . ." Halley's immediate reaction was to disavow her crush on Wade. But Sofee hadn't bought it on Saturday, so why would she buy it now? And why was her first reaction to lie to her friend? Halley paused, but Sofee was on a roll.

"Well, then she's totally breaking friend code by even *talking* to him!" Sofee declared. "She's nothing more than a skanky guy-thief—a stealer of crushes. Right?"

Uh-oh. This morning Sofee had claimed to be *over* Wade. So did this mean Halley would be breaking friend code if she went out with him—or was Sofee just looking out for Halley's feelings?

Ten minutes ago, Halley had thought a stupid cheerleading routine was complicated. But the wounded look on Sofee's face made Halley realize that perfecting a basket toss was the least of her worries.

Cheer factor

$\mathcal{A}$valon glanced over at the girls' locker room door and stuffed her sweaty practice clothes into her green Puma gym bag. She sat down on the bench and shot another look at the door, willing Halley to enter. The clock above the wall-to-wall mirrors showed that it was after five o'clock. *What* was taking Halley so long? How many art assignments could she possibly be discussing with her freak-of-the-week friend? Hadn't she realized Sofee was *so last season*?

"Well, *that* completely sucked," Avalon heard someone say from the next row of lockers over. It had to be Sydney. Before they'd become friends, Avalon had secretly named her the Cheerhuahua because of her yappy voice. Luckily, the high pitch had become less annoying as Avalon got to know the co-captain better.

"It didn't just suck," said another voice Avalon recognized

as belonging to Gabby Velasquez. "It was a joke. I seriously hope we don't have to cheer at *games* with this pseudo-squad. We'll be laughed off the field."

Avalon stiffened. Sydney and Gabby obviously thought the locker room was empty. She slowed her breathing and listened.

"Did Brianna seem like she was struggling out there?" Sydney asked so quietly that Avalon had to strain to hear her.

"What do you mean?" Gabby demanded. "I thought she was doing the best she could, but those losers just didn't get it."

Losers?

"I don't know." Sydney sighed. "Style Snarks said Brianna wasn't good enough to lead the new team. That was all I could think about out there."

Huh? Avalon struggled to remain quiet as her heartbeat quickened. *That's not what we said. . . .*

"Seriously?" Gabby practically hissed. "How could they say something like that?"

"I dunno, but you should read it," Sydney said flatly. "I mean, people are talking. . . ."

"Whatever," Gabby snapped. "Brianna's an awesome captain."

"I agree, but . . ." Sydney paused. Avalon could hear the co-captain practically hyperventilating. She held her breath and pressed herself against a locker to get as close to Sydney as possible. "It's just that combining the teams is a *huge* job. And it's our first competition. And . . . well . . . if Avalon hadn't helped lead the gymnasts today, practice would have been even *worse*. . . ."

Oh. My. God. Avalon had to get out of the locker room before anybody caught her eavesdropping. She crept toward the door, taking the route through the gym. When she got into the main lobby, she finally let herself breathe normally again.

"Hey!" Avalon heard a familiar voice and turned to see Brianna marching down the hall toward her. Her cheeks were red and blotchy and her eyes were burning like dark, hot coals. Had she been crying?

"Oh, hey, Bree."

"You and Halley sure bolted out of practice quickly today." Now Brianna looked more angry than sad. Avalon had never seen her friend look so possessed. "But I guess that's what I'd expect after you let Halley trash me on Style Snarks," Brianna continued.

"Huh?" But Avalon knew where this was heading. She'd heard enough in the locker room. She just wished she'd had more of a chance to prepare her rebuttal. "Well, first of all, I don't *let* Halley do anything. She's pretty independent. What are you saying, exactly?"

"'*With the right person in charge*'?" Brianna mimicked a high, patronizing voice. A group of boys made light whistling noises as they passed by, but quickly quieted down when they saw the look on Brianna's face.

"Um . . ." Avalon tried to compose herself and explain the post. But the harder she tried to come up with the right words, the more she tripped over them. "The thing is . . . Well. I was just, I mean, Halley was just trying to tell everyone to vote for—"

"And what about Kimberleigh asking who the captain was?" Brianna cut Avalon off. She was tugging at her multicolored scarf so hard that Avalon feared she might do serious damage to her neck. "She was standing right next to Halley. And Kimberleigh is so not the type to make a power play like that all on her own. Halley's obviously trying to take me down."

Avalon desperately wanted to defend her best friend, to tell Brianna that it was because of Halley that the gymnasts had voted to merge the teams. But that would mean admitting the blog post had been her idea. How had it gone so terribly wrong? Brianna was clearly looking to make someone her nemesis, and the last thing Avalon—or the team—needed was an intercheerleader feud.

"Look, Bree, let me talk to Halley," Avalon finally said. "I'm sure it'll all work out."

"How many times can you make the same promise in one day?" Brianna shot back tersely as her lips began to tremble and her eyes welled up with tears.

As much as Avalon hated that Brianna was accusing Halley and Avalon of conspiracy and sabotage when they'd only been trying to help, her heart suddenly went out to the cheer captain. Her friend—the girl she could always count on for her positive energy—was totally cracking under the pressure of today's cheertastrophe. It was turning her into a scary, neurotic ball of angst, a poster girl for Prozac, and not exactly what most people would consider a capable leader.

"Twice, I guess," Avalon said softly. Then she stepped forward and gave Brianna's arm a quick but heartfelt squeeze. "And I really do mean it, Bree. I *am* going to talk to Halley."

Avalon offered Brianna one last sympathetic glance before heading through the school lobby and out into the front courtyard, where she saw Abigail Brandon's Mercedes CLK convertible parked in the circular drive. Fortunately, Halley— still in her workout clothes—was sitting in the backseat with Pucci. Avalon breathed a sigh of relief and rushed over to the car. She'd never been so happy to see the familiar face of her BFF. But then she remembered: Somebody *had* voted against the merger. It couldn't have been Halley, could it . . . ?

Let's make a deal

*H*alley could finally feel the stress of the day melting away as frothy bubbles of salt water tickled her bare toes. She watched the sun dipping into the ocean, while dark silhouettes of early evening surfers and swimmers bobbed against the gray-blue sky.

"Alone at last," Halley said to Avalon as Pucci bounded over and dropped her bright pink Puppy Wubba Kong on the wet shore. Halley picked up the Kong before the water could sweep it away and tossed it back down the beach for Pucci to chase.

"Seriously." Avalon shook her head dramatically. "Could this day have been more insane?"

"Oh, it gets crazier," Halley said.

"Really?" Avalon lowered her black D&G sunglasses and looked, intrigued, into Halley's eyes. Then she broke into a huge smile. "Ohmygod! Mr. Huggies!"

Halley turned to see a little bald man who had become a La Jolla legend—at least in Halvalon's world—racing along the shoreline. Everywhere they went, he seemed to suddenly pop into view, always power-walking but never seeming to arrive at his destination. Whether they were on their bikes, driving through town with their parents, or walking on the beach, there he was, wearing nothing but a saggy pair of white running shorts and a battered pair of sneakers. Although years of overexposure to the sun had turned his skin as brown and cracked as a vintage Louis Vuitton suitcase, he still looked like an overgrown baby in need of a diaper change. After about a hundred sightings, Avalon had decided to name him Mr. Huggies. The nickname still made Halley laugh.

"Diaper Dude!" Halley giggled. "I haven't seen him in ages."

"I know." Avalon nodded. "I was kind of going through sun-dried-infant withdrawal."

Halley laughed so hard she snorted. She was finally completely relaxed. She grabbed Avalon's hand and pulled her up toward the jagged cliffs, where they sat down on the soft sand littered with dark, dry bits of seaweed and broken shells. They both giggled as they watched Pucci make friends with a black Lab and try to intercept the tennis ball a bleached-blond skater boy was hurling down the beach.

"Our puppy is *such* a flirt." Halley smiled. She inhaled

deeply, taking comfort in the evening beach smell—warm and salty, with a lingering hint of suntan lotion. Then she looked over at her best friend, every bit the SoCal beauty with her long blond hair cascading down over one sun-kissed shoulder.

"Okay, so I've been trying to tell you something all day." Halley scooped up a handful of sand, then poured the grains back to the ground. When Avalon looked over, Halley quickly blurted, "Wade asked me to hang out on Friday! He said he likes me back!"

"Really?" Avalon took off her sunglasses, allowing Halley to see the setting sun glimmering in her golden brown eyes. "What happened *exactly*? And *when*?"

The words fell out of Halley's mouth faster than the sand sifting through her fingers.

"He found me this morning and told me he couldn't stop thinking about what happened at the party, and he said he feels the same way, and it's all thanks to you for singing that song and"—Halley paused and gulped—"and I just can't believe it's really happening!"

"Hal!" Avalon's smile looked like it might take over her entire face. "Do you know how amazing that is?"

"Uh-huh." Halley hooked a lock of dark hair behind each ear and kept her hands clenched on either side of her head as she widened her eyes at her best friend.

"Wow." Avalon puckered her lips and blew, but she'd

never quite mastered whistling, so it sounded more like a broken teakettle. "That's definitely crazy."

Now that the big reveal was out, Halley felt on edge again. She'd shared only the good half of the news. Plus, she still hadn't asked Avalon why she'd been talking to Wade after practice. She wasn't quite sure how to phrase the question without sounding as crazy as Sofee had.

"Okay, confession . . ." Avalon looked menacingly at Halley, sending her heart into her throat. "I kind of already knew."

"What?" Halley wasn't sure she believed her best friend. Was this like the time Avalon had claimed to have a vision that high-waisted pants would come back a full season before they showed up in *Teen Vogue*? Because Halley was still skeptical about that little *OMG, I'm psychic!* episode. "How?"

Avalon rolled her shoulders back, puffing out her chest like a bikini model. "When you bolted off after practice, Wade fully accosted me and asked all these random questions about you."

"He *did*?" Halley's heart headed back down to its rightful place and thumped happily. "Like what?"

"Ohmygod, the boy is *obsessed* with you," Avalon revealed. "He was like—" Avalon put on her best guy voice before continuing. "—'What kind of flowers does Halley like? Is she more into emo or pop? Does she listen to Boys

Like Girls or the *High School Musical* stuff? Where does she like to eat? What's her favorite movie?'"

"Seriously?" Halley felt like she was flying, airborne with the seagulls overhead, the sounds of their caws and flapping wings mimicking her racing pulse. "So what did you say? What else did *he* say?"

"Um, I can't tell you that." Avalon laughed. "That would ruin all of Romeo's supersecret surprises!"

"AV!" Halley tried not to hyperventilate.

"Well, hello? Maybe he could have asked you himself if you'd been there. I mean, I don't exactly think he was there to find *me*." Avalon tilted her head and widened her eyes. "Seriously . . . why'd you bail?"

Ugh. Halley sucked in the sea air through her nose, pulling her knees up toward her chest and hugging her arms around them. "Um . . . Sofee's been acting a little weird lately."

"Shocker." Avalon sneered. Sofee wasn't exactly her favorite person, after all.

"No, *really*," Halley continued. "The thing is, Sofee and Wade were kind of a couple last week. Sofee found me hiding in the limo after your little karaoke performance on Saturday and told me they were dating. But right after Wade asked me out this morning, Sofee said they'd just broken up."

"Ooh! Scandal." Avalon's eyes lit up.

"*Aaav* . . . this is serious." Halley gave her best friend her most pleading look.

"Sorry." Avalon frowned apologetically and squared her shoulders, then nodded, all business. "Go on."

"Okay, well, first Sofee said she didn't care about the breakup. But then she totally overreacted when she saw Wade talking to you—like she was jealous or something." Halley extended her legs and turned to look at Avalon. "She claimed she was just upset that you would flirt with him in front of *me*, since you knew I liked him. But really? I don't think she's as over him as she says."

"Wait! Sofee thinks Wade likes *me*—or *I* like *him*?" A simultaneous look of shock, amusement, and disgust flashed across Avalon's face.

"Yup!" Halley smirked and then sighed. "The thing is, I don't know what's gonna happen with Wade."

"Well, what do you *want* to happen?" Avalon asked, taking Halley's hand earnestly.

"I want to be his girlfriend," Halley confessed without even pausing, her heartbeat quickening at the mere thought of something that amazing actually happening. "Like his full-on, serious girlfriend. I totally felt like we were connected from the day we met. But when I found out he was with Sofee it was like I finally understood where the word *heartbreak* comes from. I experienced actual, physical pain!"

Halley shook her head and looked down the beach. The sky was darkening, but a few people were still enjoying the remnants of the day. Pucci had discovered a tide pool and was splashing around with a curly redheaded toddler and her parents.

"I just wish I could find out if we're really meant to be together before Sofee has to find out about us," Halley said softly.

"Well, then, go for it!" Avalon squeezed Halley's hand and locked eyes with her. "Have that hot date on Friday and figure out if the boy's worth all this angst."

"But what if Sofee still has feelings for him?" Halley groaned. She just couldn't shake Sofee's words after cheer practice. "I mean . . . I don't want to break 'friend code' and have her hate me forever."

Avalon narrowed her eyes and slowly nodded, clearly going into objective, problem-solving mode. Classic Avalon.

"Okay, I've got a plan!" All that was missing was a lightbulb springing out of her blond head. "I'll be your decoy."

"What do you mean?" Halley's face clouded over.

"Well, Sofee already thinks Wade's into me. So I'll pretend to like him whenever she's around," Avalon explained. "If she hears me talking about how much I *adore* him, or sees me with him like today, she'll be so distracted that she'll never suspect he's interested in *you*."

"But"—Halley inhaled deeply, unsure—"that sounds so deceptive."

"No, it sounds so *brilliant*," Avalon insisted. "It'll give you the time you need to be alone with your possible soul mate."

"Hmmm." Halley shuddered at the thought of hurting Sofee, but Avalon was right. It wasn't *Halley's* fault Wade had broken up with Sofee . . . was it? And Halley *had* liked him way before she knew Sofee was going out with him. And maybe Sofee really was over him . . . and—

"Come on!" Avalon bobbed her head from side to side excitedly, interrupting Halley's tortured mental debate. "There's no point in breaking 'friend code' with Sofee when she already hates *me*. I'll just let her hate me even more!"

"You're crazy." Halley shook her head and laughed through her nose. As usual, Avalon had come up with a plan just ridiculous enough to make sense.

Avalon raised her pale eyebrows, obviously satisfied with herself.

"All right." Halley grinned. "Let's do it." Insane as her BFF was, it was so great to have her back. They understood each other in a way nobody else possibly could. How had they ever survived a day apart?

"Okay, my turn," Avalon said. She stood up and shouted Pucci's name. The puppy raced back up the beach, her teeth holding firmly to the Kong that was now covered in greenish tide-pool slime.

"What?" Halley asked tentatively, wrapping her arms around the salty, sandy puppy. She wasn't sure she could take any more unexpected news today.

"Brianna kind of attacked me after cheer practice," Avalon announced.

"*Seriously?*" Halley's eyes narrowed. She didn't exactly need *another* reason to dislike Brianna. "What happened?"

"Well, I guess she got the wrong idea about our blog post." Avalon rolled her eyes. "She thought we were trying to take her down or something, even though we were totally trying to *support* her."

"Dude. That's ridiculous." Halley shook her head as she scratched behind Pucci's ears. "Doesn't she realize we got practically everybody to vote for the merger?"

"I guess not." Avalon sat back down and crossed her legs. "Plus, I actually heard Sydney talking about whether Brianna could handle being captain. . . ."

Classic! Brianna's own co-captain doubted her abilities? Halley smiled, but Avalon looked pained.

"And now Brianna thinks maybe you voted against the merger—*and* that you were the one who told Piggleigh to ask about a new captain," Avalon revealed, twirling a lock of hair.

"*What?* I voted *yes*, and Kimberleigh came up with that all on her own!" Halley clenched her fists and burrowed them into the sand. "Not that I'd be bummed to see Brianna step down."

"But who would replace her?" Avalon asked, wide-eyed.

"Well. Um. How about *YOU*?" Halley deadpanned. She was kidding at first, but as she thought about it, she realized it made total sense. After all, Avalon had experience with both teams. And it would be a lot more fun if she were in charge. "Seriously, you would be a much better captain."

"No way." Avalon shook her head. "I could never do that. It would *kill* Brianna if she lost the captain spot."

Halley could see the horror in Avalon's eyes, but there was a definite spark in there too. Somebody just needed to stoke the fire.

"Then allow me to present you with yet another brilliant plan!" Halley licked her lightly glossed lips eagerly, her head swimming with possibilities. "Since you're going to be my Wade decoy . . . and Brianna already thinks I'm trying to take her down . . ."

"No! Shut *up*!" Avalon glowered at Halley in a way that really said, *I'm all ears—please continue.*

Halley grinned. "Av, I'll just act like I'm still totally opposed to being a cheerleader, which, hello? Not much of a stretch. I'll ignore Brianna and mess up the cheers and defy the pep squad code of conduct at every turn—but *you'll* come to Brianna's defense and force me into line. Then, right when we're about to vote for our new fearless leader, I'll nominate you, and you'll take the whole team to a championship victory!"

Halley had to admit, even *she* was a little excited about the cheer competition now—if not for herself, then at least for Avalon.

Avalon shook her head in mock protest, but Halley knew this game all too well. Avalon loved feeling needed. And Halley actually enjoyed playing along.

"Come on! The team needs you! Where's that mean Greene fighting machine?" Halley screamed, jumping to her feet and daring Avalon to race as she bolted down the sand. Pucci barked and quickly sped ahead of Halley, bounding toward the edge of the water.

Halley ran hard, letting the early evening wind whip through her wavy dark hair, excitement pushing her forward. Just when her legs started burning from the sprint, she heard Avalon behind her and felt her grab the back of Halley's lavender hoodie, wrestling her to the ground.

"Okay, I'm in!" Avalon declared as the girls lay there on the sand, panting even harder than Pucci. "But there's just one problem."

"What?" Halley propped herself up on her elbows and looked at Avalon.

"We can't be friends anymore," Avalon announced soberly. "I mean, at least not in public."

"Why not?" Halley asked, hoping her best friend was just being her usual, unnecessarily melodramatic self.

"Because," Avalon explained, "if *you're* messing with Brianna, I'll have to support her. And if *I'm* flirting with Wade, you'll have to comfort Sofee and be super-mad at *me*. Meaning"—Avalon actually shuddered—"we have to be faux enemies."

"Wow." Halley shook her head gravely. She thought about how hard it would be to pretend to hate the person who meant the most to her in the world. Then she sat up straight and looked her best friend in the eyes. "Wait, Av, this is *beyond* perfect! We can announce it on Style Snarks! We'll say we broke up . . . *AGAIN*—"

"Not that *that* will surprise anyone," Avalon interjected.

"—and then we can totally go along with all the Team Halley and Team Avalon stuff and even say really mean things about each other in our blog posts." Halley laughed. "It'll be *awesome!*"

"Um, why do you seem a little *too* excited about this?" Avalon asked with a hint of concern.

"*Because*," Halley gushed, "when I'm mean to you, you'll know I'm really being mean *for* you—and vice versa. It's one more thing that'll make Halvalon the most exclusive unit ever."

Halley was completely stoked. This was so much better than a Style Snarks PR campaign! She watched as Avalon finally processed everything. Exhilaration shone in her best friend's brown eyes. Even Pucci's dark, wet mouth was curled up in a slobbery, enthusiastic smile. Halley knew that as long as they had each other, there was nothing they couldn't accomplish. They were one big, happy—and ever so slightly cunning—family.

The Style Snarks

DON'T GET DRESSED WITHOUT US!

Fall Out, Girl!

posted by halley: wednesday, october 1, at 7:03 a.m.

Well, fashionistas, the rumors are true: Halvalon is officially O-V-E-R. Like plaid and stripes, black and brown, sandals and socks . . . we may look awesome separately, but together we totally clash. Of course, this blog isn't about us, it's about YOU—and therefore, the fashion coverage will continue, uninterrupted.

So let's talk about FALL: Crisp autumn days, vibrantly colored leaves, and cute clothes galore—if, that is, you don't take some of the season's supposed trends too seriously. Just so you know, here are my top three fall fashion NOs:

1. **Leg warmers.** Seriously? They weren't even a good idea when our parents wore them. They went out of style once for a reason. And arm warmers? A MAYBE at best. Only someone truly rocking can pull that look off.

2. **Hot pants.** The most inappropriately named eyesore on and off the runway, these are neither hot nor pants. Trust me on this.

3. **Gladiator sandals.** Sorry, people, but they were a VERY. PASSING. FAD. Summer's over, so send them back to Spartacus or whoever and move on. When in Rome, okay, go for it. But guess what? You're *NOT IN ROME.* Duh!

So there you have it. Just because *Teen Vogue* says it's hot doesn't mean it's appropriate for the halls of SMS. Your tragic-wear is making my eyes hurt.

Word to your closet,
Halley Brandon

COMMENTS (76)

LOL! Good call on the gladiators. Ick. The ones Avalon was wearing the other day were SO last season. And I'll give U one more thing: Team Halvalon sure is good at doing the splits. ☺

posted by hotterthanu **on** 10/1 at 7:19 a.m.

Whoa. I'm getting whiplash trying to keep up with you guys and all your makeups and breakups. You are so tabloidalicious. So, um, go Team Halley! This column rocks. Love the advice. Hot pants are especially scary. EW!

posted by superstyleme **on** 10/1 at 7:28 a.m.

U go, girl. I knew you'd wake up and realize your "BFF" is still a full-on backstabber. Team Halley 4 Life!

posted by madameprez **on 10/1 at 7:31 a.m.**

Why don't U give it up? Hot pants and leg warmers are AWESOME—especially 2gether. GO, TEAM AVALON! Down with Team Halley!

posted by cheeriously **on 10/1 at 7:39 a.m.**

News attitude

"What I *hope* you're getting from all this," Miss Frey lectured, "is that a true reporter always remembers there are no new stories—just new angles."

Halley sat at her desk in the cyberjournalism villa, listening to her super-sophisticated teacher talk about the difference between fresh ideas and fresh *spin*. As a former *Elle* intern who'd been rumored to have had power lattes with Marc Jacobs and Donatella Versace, Miss Frey had always been an inspiration to Halvalon. But ever since their column had been disqualified from the *Daily* competition, things hadn't quite been the same in class. Now, no matter how much of a Yes she was with her shoulder-length chestnut hair, dark-rimmed Prada glasses, and lime green checkerboard Diane von Furstenberg wrap dress, Miss Frey had lost her mystique.

To make matters much, much worse, as one of their penalties for cyberbullying in their competition posts, Halley and Avalon had been demoted from reporters to so-called research editors. It was the worst gig in journalism, especially when it involved fact-checking the alleged "news" penned by Margie and Olive, who didn't waste any time in torturing Halley and Avalon relentlessly. As payback, Avalon had suggested they add a little fun to the Disease of the Day columns. So the girls had decided to trade checking facts for inventing—and replacing—them. It was only a matter of time before Margie and Olive noticed the, um, *improvements* in their writing.

"So while I run next door to re*fresh* my coffee, please start reviewing tomorrow's articles with a *fresh* attitude," Miss Frey concluded. "As you do that, think about how you might throw something unique or surprising into the mix."

Chairs screeched, students chattered, and fingertips tapped furiously on keyboards as a wadded-up piece of pink paper hit Halley in the head. She glared over at Avalon, the obvious source of the attack. Step one in their new public image of full-on Halvalon hate was to openly antagonize each other at school. And cyberjournalism class was the perfect opportunity. But Avalon gave her a look that signaled this note was very real. Halley covertly picked up the crumpled rose-colored ball and smoothed it out. On the page was a picture of two sad-looking little insects—one long and skinny

and the other small and round—with the words MARGIE &
OLIVE: DANCING WITH THE PESTS!

Before Halley could laugh, the vomitrocious sound of
thrift-store clogs shuffling across the polished floor assaulted
her Tiffany-studded ears.

"Hey there, Style Snarksss!" Margie hissed the words
like a snake—fitting for someone so pale-skinned, green-
eyed, and impossibly tall. "Our column's ready for your fact-
checking."

"Ohmygod, hey! I almost didn't recognize you guys without your mosquito suits on!" Avalon giggled, sliding into the
desk next to Halley.

Halley resisted the urge to laugh and balled up the note
in her hand. She shot a fake irritated look at Avalon.

"Laugh all you like," Margie said haughtily, snapping her
head in Avalon's direction. "We know you're just jealous."

"Yeah!" Olive quipped in typical sidekick style.

"Oh, and could you *pleeease* leave your own notes out this
time?" Margie droned. "We're on deadline and don't have
time to edit out your ignorant asides."

"Are you implying your last story sucked because of me?
Because I suggest you point the finger at yourselves . . . or
her." Avalon waved her left hand disgustedly at Halley while
glaring up at Margie.

Halley channeled all her rage at Margie and Olive into an
indignant "Pffft!" directed at her best friend.

"She's not implying anything," Olive retorted, silver braces accentuating her fish lips. "She's telling you to get your shallow little noses out of *Us Weekly* and do your *fact-checking* job instead of trying to turn our column into a replica of your pathetic excuse for a blog!"

Halley began chewing on a dark purple pinkie nail to keep from saying something she might regret. But Avalon preferred confrontation to nervous habits.

"You're so deluded," Avalon scoffed, aggressively straightening her tight pink TEAM AVALON T-shirt. Halley appreciated that her best friend's commitment to their fake feud extended to her fashion choices. "Besides, the only things worth reading in your ridiculous Disease of the Day columns are our fun facts."

"Facts are neither fun—*nor facts*—if they're completely made up!" Margie snapped. Her black helmet of hair looked like it might pop right off her head.

"What's *that* supposed to mean?" Avalon demanded, fiery gold flecks dancing angrily in her brown eyes.

Halley wanted to add something to the conversation, but watching Avalon go at it was way too much fun. Besides, she couldn't exactly back her up in public.

"Let me translate it for you, shopaholic," Olive spat, literally, as the overhead lights reflected off her metal mouth. "Only someone who cares more about clothes than closing the poverty gap would add a celebrity sidebar to an important piece about the worldwide meningitis epidemic."

"Olive, this is pointless," Margie barked, dropping two sheets of coffee-stained paper onto the keyboard of Avalon's iMac, and a similarly stained article onto Halley's keyboard. "We have lives to save."

Avalon cackled as Margie and Olive turned and lurched toward the magazine racks in the back of the room, probably hoping to grab the latest issue of *ElleNerd*.

David Cho—Brianna's younger brother and the *Daily* entertainment reporter—joined in Avalon's laughter while continuing to type furiously. Avalon wrinkled her nose to acknowledge the support, but Halley just shook her head. She wished she could tell Avalon how awesome she had just been, but that would have to wait until they were alone. Now instead of getting down to the business of fact-checking an article about a disease that had died out around the time of powdered wigs, she launched into a fight—just like they'd agreed last night.

"Great job," Halley quipped antagonistically. "I told you we should have left the column alone."

"Oh, please," Avalon shot back. "You were the one who said we should add Lindsay Lohan and Ashlee Simpson for no reason."

Halley shook her head fervently. "Oh no, that was all you."

"Is there a problem here, girls?" Miss Frey towered over

Halley and Avalon, looking more worried than angry as she took a sip of coffee, the steam from her mug fogging up her glasses.

Halley hadn't even noticed the teacher come back into the villa. "Oh . . . um . . . no," Halley stammered. "Sorry, Miss Frey. We were just trying to figure out how to put a fresh spin on mononucleosis."

"Well, then, I'll leave you to it!" Miss Frey smiled and walked back to her desk.

Halley took out her favorite red fact-checking pencil, more convinced than ever that a fake public feud was exactly the key to solidifying the Halvalon reunion for good. As she began reading Margie and Olive's column about the ways that sharing things can make you sick, she was tempted to just put a big red X through the whole thing. After all, the more she and Avalon shared, the more indestructible they became. That would definitely be a fact worth writing about—if it weren't quite so Style Snarks confidential.

The Style Snarks

DON'T GET DRESSED WITHOUT US!

Crimes of Fashion

posted by halley: thursday, october 2, at 7:13 a.m.

Have you ever thrown on an outfit thinking it was perfectly acceptable, only to later walk by a mirror and realize, "OMG! How did I leave the house looking like *that*?" Perhaps you didn't even realize wearing a tight T-shirt with your own name plastered inappropriately across your massive chest would be a bad idea until you heard the rumblings of ridicule behind your back. Whatever the case, the simple fact is, you've found yourself in the middle of a fashion crime scene and, as tragedy would have it, you're both the victim *and* the perpetrator. What can you do? I recommend the following:

1. **Run for cover.** Head for the nearest bathroom stall, lock the door, and do not emerge until the sun goes down—at which point the dark of night will serve as the ideal cloak for concealing your fashion transgression. This is a particularly useful tactic for tanorexics, who aren't as easy to see after hours.

2. **Ramp it up.** Grab your oversize sunglasses, throw on a hat (especially important to cover up a bad bleach job!), and

pretend you're a celebrity *trying* to make it into the pages of *Us Weekly*'s Fashion Police column.

3. **Report it.** Seriously. Call 911 and tell them it's an emergency. (Because it is—a *fashion* emergency!) Then lie down on the ground and wait for the ambulance to arrive. It's the fastest way to win the pity of the people. They'll be less concerned about your clothes if they think you're ailing more than the awful outfit you accidentally threw on.

Just remember: One fashion felony is forgivable. Two is asking for trouble. But three strikes? You're OUT.

Word to your closet,

Halley Brandon

COMMENTS (76)

LMAO! Could not believe the *other* Snark wore that T-shirt yesterday. Conceited much? She shouldn't be. Cuz it was SO. NOT. FLATTERING. ☹

posted by hautestuff **on 10/2 at 7:22 a.m.**

The Snark is ON! I'm seriously liking the edge on this column. I knew u 2 were better apart. lolz

posted by tuffprincess **on 10/2 at 7:31 a.m.**

Better not kiss and make up, girls. Find out why in Margie and Olive's Disease of the Day column <u>here</u>.

posted by dissect_this **on 10/2 at 7:34 a.m.**

Sent: Thursday, October 2, 7:37 a.m.
From: Halley Brandon <hallyeah@yahoo.com>
To: Wade Houston <deadromeo13@gmail.com>
Subject: Hi. ☺

Hey,

So sorry I've been outta touch. Crazy week,
y'know? Anyway, I got your message about La
Cucaracha tomorrow and I will totally be there.
Can't wait!

TTYL,
Hal

PS: Let's not tell anyone about this—at least not yet.
Especially Sofee! (Not that you would, right?) ☺

Wade Houston, we have a problem

"*D*ad, that was amazing." Halley sopped up the last drops of sauce from her five-cheese lasagna with a final bite of sourdough and wiped her mouth with the back of her hand. "You should so audition for *America's Next Top Chef*!"

"Uhhh, it's *America's Next Top* Model, fashion freak." Tyler guffawed. "The food show is just *Top Chef*."

"Whatever." Halley rolled her eyes at her brother as she located one more drop of sauce on her plate, wiped it up with her finger, and tapped it onto her tongue.

"Of course, if you keep eating like that, *you'll* have to audition for *The Biggest Loser*." Tyler snorted, shooting a blob of tomato out of his mouth and down onto his already stained GEOLOGY ROCKS shirt.

"Oh, but you already *are* the biggest loser!" Halley sneered with sisterly affection.

"Guys, if you're going to insult each other"—Abigail Brandon tried to put on her stern-mom face—"at least try a little harder than reality TV."

"Way to lay down the law, babe." Charles smiled at Abigail like she was a supermodel—which she sort of was in her cobalt Michael Stars jersey tank dress, with her long auburn hair pulled up into a loose ponytail. Her skin was so smooth and her eyes so crystal blue and heavily lashed that she didn't even need to wear makeup.

"Well, how about this one: Keep up the disses and you'll be doing the *dishes*!" Abigail raised her perfectly arched eyebrows at Halley and Tyler just as the doorbell rang.

"I'll get it!" Halley jumped up.

"No, *I'll* get it!" Tyler pushed Halley out of the way as he bolted past her to the frosted-glass front door, flinging it open.

Halley rushed up and peeked around Tyler's shoulder so she could see who was outside.

"*Sofee* . . . ?" Halley's friend stood on the gray slate front steps, leaning her red beach cruiser against the wall. In her charcoal tube top, dark-wash denim mini, and silver flats, she wasn't exactly dressed for a chilly evening bike ride.

"Hey, Hal." Sofee sniffed. Her eyes were red and puffy. "You busy?"

"Oh . . . um . . ." Halley turned to look back at the dining room, where Tyler was now rejoining their parents at the table. "Mom?" she called from the door.

"Yeah, kiddo?"

"Sofee's here. Can I help you guys clean up later?"

"Sure! No worries!"

Halley led Sofee upstairs to her room and sat down on the orange circular rug in the middle of the hardwood floor. Sofee collapsed into the tan suede beanbag in the corner. Before Halley could even ask what was up, tears started streaming down her friend's face. And within about thirty seconds, a few quiet sniffles turned into all-out sobbing. *What the . . . ?* Sofee had yet to say a word. Halley had helped Avalon through her share of breakdowns, but this was different. This was a totally in-control rock chick extraordinaire. And Wade's ex. *Awkward, party of two?*

Halley stood up and grabbed a box of Kleenex from beside her bed to hand to Sofee. She'd read in September's *CosmoGIRL!* that small gestures could be more powerful than words when dealing with friends in crisis.

"Thanks." Sofee honked into a tissue. Halley always wondered how people with nose rings sneezed without hurting themselves, but realized this probably wasn't the time to ask. "S-s-s-sorry I'm such a mess," Sofee stuttered through a sob.

"Don't worry about it." Halley sat back down on her rug and frowned empathetically. When Sofee raised her head with a self-conscious half smile, Halley felt like she could finally ask what this was all about. So she did.

"Wade and I just had a huge fight at rehearsal." Sofee's

full, glossed lips trembled as she said the words. "I accused him of starting the Dead Romeos just so he could hook up with unnaturally boobular Barbies."

Trying to hide a giggle, Halley stood and walked over to her desk. She sat down and lit one of the triple-wicked Voluspa candles that the Moms had given Halley and Avalon for Chrismukkah the year before. As she inhaled the sweet smell of citrus, she hoped it would help Sofee relax.

"Of course he totally denied it," Sofee continued bitterly, dabbing at her nose and tossing the tissue into the shiny orange trash can a few feet away.

"But I thought you were over him . . ." Halley said softly as she ran her fingers through her dark wavy locks.

"I *am* over him!" Sofee's voice gained strength with each word. "I mean, guys are *such* jerks. And Wade is risking the entire future of our band."

"Oh." Halley leaned back in her egg chair. *CosmoGIRL!* had also suggested asking questions instead of offering solutions. So by prying, she would actually *help* Sofee work out her feelings. It wasn't selfish at all. Or so she told herself. "But how would Wade's liking Barbies hurt the band? Are Evan and Mason angry that he broke up with you?"

"I'm not even sure they knew we were together." Sofee got up from the beanbag and walked over to Halley's balcony door, staring out the window. "But history is littered with bands on the brink of success, only to be destroyed by the bimbo-distraction factor. How can Wade treat that possibility so casually?"

"Hmmm." Halley felt a little queasy. Was Sofee serious? If this was true, was Halley the real bimbo in this scenario? And why hadn't Sofee worried about *inner-band dating* tearing the band apart? Halley couldn't help but wonder if this was really about the band or about Sofee's feelings for her ex. "Well, is there anything I can, you know, *do*?"

"You know what, Hal?" Sofee said, walking toward Halley, her head held high. When she got to the egg chair, she stared down into Halley's eyes like she could see inside her head—kind of the way Wade sometimes did. "You're already doing it."

Shoot. She knows. "I am?" Halley asked cautiously.

"Yeah," Sofee said softly, and strutted back over to the balcony door, then spun around to face Halley. "I mean, I'm not sure I've ever had a friend like you—somebody who totally gets me and has my back. Anytime I feel like things suck, I think about how much fun we had at art camp and how supportive you've been of me and the Dead Romeos and . . . I dunno." Sofee looked down, embarrassed. "I'm just glad you don't mind me venting all this stuff to you."

"Ohmygod, Sofee . . ." Halley was floored. She wanted to give her friend a hug and protect her from all the evil boys in the world. She'd been in such awe of this mature, cool, amazingly talented girl since camp that she'd never really thought about how much *she* meant to *Sofee*. Even Avalon didn't talk about her feelings like that. Maybe it was an artist thing. Musicians were just so . . . *intense*. But before Halley could tell Sofee how important their friendship was to her, too, the moment was interrupted.

"Hey, girls!"

Halley and Sofee both looked over to see Tyler standing at the bedroom door. He had changed out of his sauce-stained tee and into a retro-hip black-and-white shirt with the name NORM embroidered on the pocket. "Anybody interested in hitting the bowling alley?"

Sofee gave Halley an amused-quizzical look.

"Tyler just got a Wii and he's become a little obsessed with bowling—not that he's managed to beat me yet," Halley explained with a grin.

"Um, the name's Norm," Tyler corrected, running a finger along his pocket.

"Oh, sorry . . . *Norm*." Halley giggled.

"Well, good to meet you, Norman!" Sofee's face relaxed into a wide smile. "And I *love* bowling—especially the shoes."

"Then check *these* babies out," Tyler said, launching himself onto Halley's bed and holding up his legs to show off a pair of hideous black-and-red suede shoes.

"Ohmygod, Ty—sorry—*Norm*, aren't you taking this game a little far?" Halley laughed, although the shoes were kind of awesomely ugly.

"Hal, bowling is not just a game," Tyler deadpanned. "It's a *lifestyle*."

"I didn't realize the Wii knew what kind of shoes you were wearing." Sofee widened her dark eyes innocently.

"Well, the shoes aren't exactly required," Tyler noted, swatting his floppy brown hair out of his eyes. "But it makes the whole experience that much more real. Like you're actually *there*, rollin' strikes and taking names!"

Sofee was clearly fighting back a grin.

"And honestly," Tyler continued, grabbing his upper arm as he flexed his nonexistent muscle, "my right bicep is really bulking up."

"I bet!" Sofee choked down a laugh as she leaned against the glass door. "I've heard it's a pretty awesome workout. But the real question is: Do you have Guitar Hero?"

Halley looked over at her brother faux-sympathetically as his face fell.

"No, not yet." Tyler shook his head, defeated. "It's at the top of my wish list."

"Well, when you get that, I'll be here kicking your butt daily." Sofee tilted her head with an edgy scowl and pumped one of her slender arms in the air, causing her stack of silver bracelets to jingle like a tambourine.

"Better watch out, Norm," Halley cautioned with a grin. "That's not an idle threat."

"Oooh, I'm trembling!" Tyler clutched the sides of his face in mock fear.

"Well, could you tremble somewhere else?" Halley asked. After all, Sofee hadn't come over to play video games.

"What about bowling?" Tyler whined.

"Later, Norm . . ." Halley said firmly, getting up from her desk and marching over to drag her brother off the bed.

"Promise . . . ?" Tyler begged as Halley shut the door in his face.

"Promise!" she shouted as she turned back to Sofee, who was looking out the window again.

"Hey . . . are you expecting another visitor?" Sofee pushed Halley's sliding door open and walked out onto the balcony, which wrapped around the front of the ultramodern house and provided a perfect view of the street.

"Uh, no." Halley crept outside behind Sofee and looked over her friend's shoulder.

Ohmygod. Wade was riding his bike straight toward them! While Sofee continued to stare at the street, Halley stealthily dashed inside, grabbed her phone off her desk, and sent a lightning-fast *911. Sofee here. Wade outside* text to Avalon. Luckily, she could text faster than she could do pretty much anything.

Look at your phone, look at your phone. . . . Halley scrunched her eyes closed and sent out intense BFF vibes as she slipped back out onto the patio. But Wade was getting closer to

Halley's house by the second. How was she going to explain this to Sofee? Had her front door sprouted a WELCOME, DEAD ROMEOS sign on it in the past hour?

"Wade!" Avalon's voice squealed through the night air, loud enough for the entire neighborhood to hear. She skipped out her front door and raced down her steps just as Wade was about to ride past the Greenes' driveway.

Sofee gasped. Halley did too. They both leaned as far over Halley's balcony as they could without being detected. Halley was suddenly grateful for Avalon's flair for the dramatic. She was giving a truly memorable performance. Beneath the yellow glow of the street lamps, Halley could see the flirtatious smile on Avalon's lips. She could hear her giggling and cooing. It almost made Halley jealous. But mostly, it just made her proud.

Finally, Avalon leaned in, hugged Wade close, and then shook her pin-straight blond hair adoringly as she waved him onto his bike. Watching Wade ride down the street, Avalon effortlessly tossed out the pièce de résistance and blew a kiss to his retreating back.

"Wow," Sofee said, drawing in her breath as she turned away from the balcony and headed inside.

Halley braced herself for a tirade—or a sob-fest to end all sob-fests—and followed Sofee into the bedroom.

"So, have you started the watercolor project for art?" Sofee asked casually, grabbing her black army satchel from beside Halley's beanbag and heading toward the bedroom door.

"Oh, um . . ." Halley quickly shifted gears. Was that all Sofee was going to say about what they'd just seen? "No. I'm so bad with brushes, you know? I'm way more of a sketch artist."

"Yeah. Me too." Sofee gave Halley a forced smile and smoothed down a few of the purple streaks in her hair. "I should probably go work on it, though."

"Yeah." Halley walked Sofee out of the bedroom and down to the front door. "I'm so not in the mood for homework, but whatever. It's got to be done."

"I guess." Sofee shrugged. Her eyes looked sad again. But her tears had been replaced by defeat.

"Sofee . . ." Halley finally said tentatively, placing a hand on her friend's bare shoulder. She didn't want to let homework be the last thing she mentioned after their heart-to-heart, not to mention what they'd witnessed. "Don't you want to talk about what just happened?"

"Yeah." Sofee nodded and narrowed her onyx eyes. "Definitely. But I kind of need to process it first. And I figure you probably do too."

"Oh. Right." Halley opened the front door and watched Sofee wheel her bike down to the curb. "Well, call me if you need anything, okay?" Halley shouted.

"Totally!" Sofee yelled back as she began riding away.

The minute the red bike was out of sight, Halley raced back upstairs and speed-dialed Avalon.

"Dude!" Halley exhaled when Avalon picked up. "I don't know what just happened, but thank you."

"Oh, please." Halley could hear Avalon smiling on the other end of the line. "It was fun."

"So what *did* just happen?" Halley collapsed onto her bed, deciding she should probably be sitting for this.

"Well, your lovesick lead singer was hoping for a video-game playdate." Avalon giggled. "But I told him you were downtown at an art exhibit, checking out pictures of guitars for him!"

Halley exhaled hard and shook her head. She wanted to run over to Avalon's house and hug her. She wanted to run over to Wade's house and kiss him. But she also wanted to chase after Sofee and make sure she was really okay.

The fact that Wade had come over, unannounced, proved how much he wanted to be with Halley. Didn't it? But did the fact that Sofee had come over, distraught, mean that she was still into Wade? Halley couldn't be sure. The only thing she knew for certain was that Avalon had officially set the heart of their plan into motion. No turning back now.

The Style Snarks

DON'T GET DRESSED WITHOUT US!

Fashion Rocks!

posted by avalon: friday, october 3, at 7:26 a.m.

Hey, look! It's my first post since our much-buzzed-about split. Sorry I haven't checked in for a couple days! Anyway, while I took a brief hiatus from the fashion blogosphere, I realized I should thank my former BFF for one thing: helping me realize that music can be a major fashion muse. I totally get it now, so here's why the rocker look might be a total YES after all:

1. **Scary is the new sassy.** It's true. When you claim MTV as your style guru, you can basically wear anything and call it "edgy." Goth, punk, androgynous, even '50s glam. No matter how over-the-top you look, you still rock!

2. **Graphic tees are all good.** Advertising your fave band on your sleeve is a major YES this season. In fact, concert-wear never goes out of style—and the more classic, the better (bonus points for true vintage).

3. **Band guys are cute!** And I'm not talking about marching band. But if he plays an instrument or sings, he's an instant YES—even in an ugly white suit and skinny tie. I mean, hello? The Jonas Brothers drive girls wild, but be honest: Would you give them a second look if they traded their guitars for Nintendo DS Lites? Case clothed! ☺

Hope to see you all at the next hot concert. I'll be the one checking out the baby tees!

Shop on,
Avalon Greene

COMMENTS (89)

Um, poseur much? A few weeks ago you said the rocker look sucks. Either you finally grew a brain, you're a total fraud, or you're a skanky crush-stealer. I'm not sold on the brain option. Seriously. BOYCOTT TEAM AVALON, PEOPLE!

posted by rockgirrrl on 10/3 at 7:34 a.m.

I can't tell if you're kidding or not. I mean, I totally think some musicians and bands dress well, but mostly they look like they need to bathe. Repeatedly! lol

posted by superstyleme on 10/3 at 7:41 a.m.

I agree with rockgirrrl. Poseur + Fraud = Lame. Avalon =
LOSER! Sorry.

posted by jimisghost **on 10/3 at 7:50 a.m.**

Yay. Glad to see you finally realized how awesome the rock
look is. Kan another Halvalon rekonciliation be far behind?!?!?

posted by kre8ivekween **on 10/3 at 7:54 a.m.**

Take one for the team

The newly merged SMS pep squad stood at the fifty-yard line on the Pacific Middle School football field, holding an enormous GO, MIGHTY LIONS poster they'd painted during lunch. An elderly woman's voice crackled through the outdoor speakers, welcoming the Seaview Lions. The SMS football team raced through the goalposts, down to the middle of the field, and burst through the poster.

"Woo-hoo! Go, Lions!" Avalon yelled, doing a couple of high kicks and herkies. "Let's sink those Tritons!"

"All right, Tritons!" Halley screamed. "I mean, Lions? I mean, WHATEVER! Go, football players!" She mocked the moves Avalon was doing with exaggerated obnoxiousness. Then she gathered up some of the decimated poster paper and shoved it into her top in an obvious attempt to imitate Avalon's boobs. Halley proceeded to prance around the squad, squealing, "Look! I'm a *real* cheerleader now!"

"Seriously? Could you be more infantile?" Avalon practically yelled at her best friend. She smiled inwardly at the awesomeness of their performance.

"Wah! Wah! Wah!" Halley shot a super-convincing antagonistic look at Brianna and then bounded over to the SMS side of the field with most of the gymnasts laughing and following behind her. Because it was an away game, the SMS crowd was pretty sparse—mostly parents, a few teachers, and no more than a dozen students. Avalon was relieved there weren't more people to see how meek the Lions cheerleaders really were.

"Ohmygod, that's horrifying." Sydney widened her violet eyes at Avalon as they lined up and watched the Tritons' kickoff. "Do you hear what they're saying?"

Avalon strained to make out what the cheerleaders and the huge crowd of people across the field were chanting. A smile began to play on her full, C.O. Bigelow–glossed lips as she finally figured it out:

P-M-S!
Is the best!
P-M-S!
Is the best!

"Do you think they even know what they're saying?" Avalon burst out laughing. Poor Pacific Middle School!

"Oooh, *that's* mature!" Halley sneered at Avalon as she leapt by.

Avalon maintained her fake-angry glare at Halley— who looked totally adorable in the plain blue tennis skirt and gold tank top they'd been suited up with until the new competition-quality uniforms arrived. Of course, Halley had cut the bottom of her tank so it showed off her perfectly flat abs whenever she raised her arms. And she'd waited until the last possible moment to unveil her uniform—showing up to the game in a gray Marc by Marc Jacobs trench coat and suede ankle boots before changing into her standard blue Nikes. Halley stuck her tongue out, and Avalon rolled her eyes.

"So, you and Halley are really broken up again?" Sydney whispered loudly.

Avalon just nodded and glowered with as much fabricated rage as she could muster. Brianna took a few steps forward, bellowed, "Ready? Okay!" and launched into the first cheer. Avalon threw herself full force into the performance:

L-I-O-N-S!
We're Lions, we don't take no mess!
Lions, Lions, hear us roar!
Lions, Lions, watch us score!

Lions, Lions, can't be beat!
Lions, get up off your feet!
Gooooo, Lions!

It was the cheer Avalon had done when she'd made the squad a few weeks ago. That day seemed so long ago. Now, as Brianna led them in a dance sequence, Avalon felt like she'd been cheering her whole life. It came so naturally to her. Unfortunately, that wasn't the case for some of the newer squad members. Avalon glanced around nervously as Piggleigh botched a few steps and almost collided with Halley. Halley responded by messing up a few more moves on purpose. Avalon watched out of the corner of her eye as Brianna shot an angry look in Halley's direction. Distracted by Halley's screwup, Brianna kicked a few seconds early and . . .

Oh. My. God.

Brianna stumbled over one of Halley's feet and fell onto a muddy patch of grass by the players' bench. Avalon wanted to rush over to help, but the captain had always told the squad that no matter what happened, they should keep cheering. If only Brianna could follow her own direction now. Instead, she just sat there on the ground, staring up at Halley in obvious anger.

Get up, Bree. Get up! Avalon felt horrible for her friend, but was surprised at how slowly she recovered. Brianna was still the captain. This was her chance to prove herself to the squad—to brush off the mistake and get back in the action. That was what Avalon would have done, *especially* if someone like Halley tried to disregard her authority. But Brianna simply sat there.

Just when Brianna should have jumped off the ground and back into the cheer, Mitch Bauer, a stocky linebacker with weird patches of blond hair (rumor had it he lost a bet with his teammates), looked down. He cackled at Brianna and signaled to a few of the guys on the bench. Nobody in the SMS stands was paying attention to the game at this point either. Meanwhile, some of the PMS girls across the field screamed, "Have a nice trip; see you next fall!" Avalon was mortified for her friend—and for the entire squad.

Brianna looked like she was going to cry as she stared down at her perfectly pressed blue skirt, now covered in brown skid marks. Avalon knew that Brianna's mistake had been caused, at least in part, by Halley—and by their pact. Stealing a glance at her best friend, Avalon was relieved to see that Halley looked the tiniest bit remorseful. When the cheer finally ended, Avalon couldn't hold back any longer.

"Bree, are you okay?" Avalon asked with genuine concern, rushing to her friend's side. She extended her arm to help Brianna up. The PMS cheerleaders were stumbling around, pretending to trip one another.

"Yeah." Brianna took Avalon's hand and rose to her feet. She brushed herself off and scowled in Halley's direction. "No thanks to your best friend."

"Um, *ex*–best friend," Avalon corrected, glaring at Halley with the same fervor as Brianna.

"Really?" Brianna tightened the bright blue bow on her long dark ponytail and locked eyes with Avalon.

"Totally." Avalon nodded. "Didn't you see the announcement on Style Snarks?"

"I kind of decided not to read it anymore," Brianna mumbled, biting her lower lip.

Avalon couldn't blame Brianna for that. But she wondered why Brianna wasn't rising above it. A true captain, like the Bree she thought she knew and loved, would step up her game. Looking back over the last week, Avalon could see just how differently she would have led the blended team. She didn't understand how Brianna could be failing so badly to bring this squad together.

Avalon looked over at Halley and the rest of the gymnasts, who were in the middle of a bunch of random tumbling passes, and barked, "Come on, everyone! Back in line!" She gave Brianna a *we can do this* look. Brianna smiled back, weakly at first but then with more determination. Finally, together, they led a rousing performance of "We're Awesome."

Mid–toe touch, her body flying several feet off the ground,

Avalon had a sudden realization. This plan wasn't just about doing what was best for the squad anymore. Yes, they needed her. But Avalon *wanted* to be captain. She wanted to lead this team to glory. And with Halley on her side, Avalon knew nothing could stand in her way. N-O-T-H-I-N-G.

Some like it hot

*H*alley pulled her baby blue Schwinn Sierra to a stop and guided the front tire into the familiar silver bike rack. She closed her eyes and took a few deep yoga breaths as she fiddled with her lock. *Remain calm,* she repeated in her head.

Walking through the arched dark wood door of La Cucaracha, Halley inhaled the delicious smell of sizzling carne. The Mexican polka music streaming through the speakers immediately put her at ease. She and Avalon had been coming here for post–gymnastics meet dinners with their families since it was just an order-at-the-counter taco stand.

"Halley!" Olivia Martinez called out from the hostess stand. Against her strapless turquoise cotton dress, the exotically beautiful restaurant owner's dark skin glowed like the bronze artwork on the rust-colored walls.

"¡Hola!" Halley grinned and allowed herself to be scooped up into a hug. "¿Cómo estás?"

Olivia's manga-round brown eyes sparkled as she rattled off an excited stream of Spanish that Halley couldn't entirely follow. Halley just nodded happily while Olivia tossed her long black hair behind her bare shoulders, becoming more animated—and unintelligible—by the minute.

"Wow, Avalon was right." A familiar voice came from Olivia's side. Halley tried to maintain her cool when she looked over and saw Wade's dark eyes shining at her. "You *are* a regular here."

"Not just a regular," Olivia insisted, a smile playing on her lips as she looked over at Wade. "This is Halley's second home."

Wade stared at Halley so intently it made her a little dizzy. "Well," he said, "I'm honored to be a guest, then."

"*Mi casa es su casa.*" Halley shrugged and cocked her head flirtatiously, holding Wade's gaze as Olivia turned to pick up two menus.

"*¡Muchas gracias!*" Wade grinned, chasing away the last few first-date butterflies in Halley's stomach.

"Come, come!" Olivia broke through the mutual stare-fest and led Halley and Wade to the booth next to the open kitchen, where they could watch the food being prepped. Olivia gave Halley a furtive thumbs-up sign and quickly disappeared.

"You look amazing." Wade fixed his eyes on Halley again, sending shivers down her spine.

She'd gone for the casual-meets-couture look: a silky gray-and-red off-the-shoulder Gaultier tunic (thanks, Mom!) over her most comfortable pair of Seven jeans and flat Miss Sixty suede boots.

"Thanks." Halley beamed. "So do you."

She wasn't lying. Wade had a little extra pomade in his jet-black hair, and he was wearing a plaid Levi's button-down over a white T-shirt with dark red-wash jeans. Halley had never seen anyone attempt that particular shade of denim before, but he pulled it off like a true rock star.

"Thanks." Wade looked around like he was about to say something seriously private and whispered: "So, I can't believe we're eating at a place called the Cockroach. Seems like they're just asking for trouble."

"Oh, you want trouble?" Halley did her best flirty eyebrow raise as Joaquin, Olivia's nephew, plunked down a platter with fresh, hot tortilla chips and four different kinds of salsa. "Try the habañero," she suggested.

"Is that a dare?" Wade asked, casually placing an elbow on the table and resting his perfectly angular jaw in one palm.

"Do you want it to be?" Halley batted her long lashes and matched Wade's chin-in-hand maneuver.

"¡Sí!" Wade squared his shoulders and laced his fingers, extending his arms to crack his knuckles tough-guy style.

Then he grabbed a chip and dunked it into the largest of the four bowls.

"Uh, that's pico," Halley informed him, then waved an index finger toward one of the smaller bowls. "*That's* the habañero."

"I know," Wade deadpanned. "I just wanted to make sure *you* knew."

"Oh, I know," Halley assured him. "My dad *is* a gourmet chef."

"Oooh, impressive!" Wade squealed and fluttered his eyelashes just like Halley had a moment ago. His sarcasm pushed his hotness from intense to scorching. After all, mesmerizing eyes were one thing, but a sense of humor to top it off? *Muy caliente*. He picked up another chip and took an even bigger scoop from the little habañero bowl.

"You might want to ease into it," Halley suggested.

"Hmm, don't think I can handle it?" Wade tilted his head and gave Halley an exaggerated pout, waving the chip in front of his lips.

"I'm not saying that—" Halley didn't get a chance to finish her thought as Wade shoved the entire chip into his mouth. Almost immediately, his face turned as red as his jeans.

"Olivia!" Halley called out, startling a family at the next booth over.

Wade fanned his face, which was now approaching magenta. Olivia raced up with a giant pitcher of ice water and a bowl of carrots. Wade nearly knocked the silverware off the table as he reached for the water, drinking straight from the pitcher. After a few minutes of chugging water, he wiped the last few tears from his eyes and sighed.

"Wow. You weren't kidding."

"I never kid about food." Halley shook her head and frowned empathetically. "But I am sorry. I didn't mean to make you cry on our first date."

Wade laughed. "I guess being with you will be an adventure."

Was that a promise?

As much as Halley wanted to run up on the roof and shout to all of La Jolla that she was on a date with Wade, she still couldn't shake the image of Sofee crying in her room. No matter how many times she claimed to be over him, she *must* still be into Wade. Or maybe she really was just concerned about the band. One minute she was declaring all guys "jerks," but the next she was freaking out about Wade talking to Avalon. Sofee could go from blasé to bawling in sixty seconds flat. Thinking about Sofee's mixed messages was threatening to ruin the most amazing night of Halley's life. She had to do something about that, pronto.

"So . . . I don't want to make you cry again or anything." Halley smirked, lifting a dark red thumbnail up to her mouth and then dropping her hand down to the table before she could actually bite it. "But, um . . ."

"What?" Wade's face looked so beautiful in the dim candle-light of their booth, especially now that it had returned to its usual pale tone with just a hint of color under his perfect cheekbones and along his flawless nose.

"I need to know what's up with you and Sofee—or what *was* up." Halley's nerves definitely would have gotten the best of her if she hadn't been practicing that line since Tuesday.

"Ah." Wade stared down at the table and nodded slowly before looking back into Halley's eyes. "It never would have worked."

"Why not?" As relieved as she was to hear it, she needed to know more. If she was going to break friend code and date Sofee's ex, she had to have all of the details.

"Because . . ." Wade trailed off and crunched on a carrot slice thoughtfully. "I mean, Sofee rocks. But we're band-mates. We have to keep it professional. And besides"—Wade leaned forward and gently grabbed Halley's hands across the table—"I felt, like, a connection from the first second I saw you."

Ohmygod. Breathe, breathe . . . Halley reminded herself.

"I just wish I'd met you before Sofee."

¡Ay, caramba!

As Wade spoke, Halley's gloomy fog of doubt began to lift. She hadn't forgotten that first moment she'd met Wade in the hall, either. There *had* been an instant connection.

They were soul mates, and nobody—not even Sofee—could stop them from being together.

The more Halley thought about the other night, the more she decided Sofee really must be over it. If anything, she seemed more concerned about *Halley's* feelings getting hurt by the Wade-Avalon sighting. Plus, Wade was obviously more worried about intraband dating than outside distractions. So there was no fear of breaking up the Dead Romeos. Telling Sofee might not be so hard, after all! But the news had to come from Halley, not Wade.

"Okay, well . . ." Halley swallowed hard, a little thrown by how quickly things were moving. "Can we just not tell anybody about us yet—I mean, whatever 'us' means?"

Wade looked as confused as Tyler did whenever Halley talked about fashion. Or celebrities. Or pop culture in general. But he nodded anyway. And that was good enough for her. Besides, she was starving.

The rest of dinner was officially the best first date in the history of first dates. They talked about music (Wade still couldn't get over all the bands Halley's mom had worked with at Capitol Records); Wade's family (his dad was a professor, his mom was a journalist, and his little brother, Johnny, had just turned four and aspired to be the lead singer for the Wiggles); and what Wade missed about San Francisco since moving to La Jolla last month (mostly the guys in his first band—the Iambic Pentameters). By the time they finished eating, Halley was stuffed full of enchiladas, salsa . . . and true love. Wade was so gorgeous. And talented. And nice. And smart. And funny. *Le package total.* It was undeniable. They'd be SMS's cutest couple. It was almost scary how perfect they were for each other.

After Wade paid the bill (swoon!), they said good-bye to Olivia and headed out to the parking lot. Halley led Wade over to the bike rack. She knelt down to dial the combination on her pink lock, feeling her awkwardness return. Would he kiss her good night? Hug her? Invite her to walk the few blocks over to his house? All—or none—of the above?

"So . . ." Wade smiled sheepishly after Halley stood up and finally faced him. "That was really awesome."

"Yeah." Halley nodded and bit her lower lip. "How's your mouth?"

"You really wanna know?" Wade raised his dark eyebrows suggestively.

Ohmygod! Halley blushed at her unintentional flirting. But apparently Wade liked girls who accidentally made the first move, because he inched closer to her.

Don't pass out. Stay focused. This is it. The kiss.

"HEY, HEY, YOU, YOU, I DON'T LIKE YOUR GIRL-FRIEND!" Avril Lavigne screamed from somewhere in Halley's bag.

No way.

Wade almost fell onto Halley's bike as she spun around to grab her bag and locate her cell phone.

"Ugh, sorry . . ." Halley tossed a glance at Wade and then looked down at the screen. *Who* was interrupting the most romantic moment of her life?

A text from Avalon:

How's my date with Wade going? ☺

Well, it was going fine . . . ! Nice timing, BFF. ☹

The Style Snarks

DON'T GET DRESSED WITHOUT US!

Stay cool; look hot.

posted by avalon: saturday, october 4, at 9:39 a.m.

You wouldn't know it's fall by the way the heat keeps threatening to burn us to a crisp here in lovely La Jolla. So I figured it was time to give you a few tips for staying cool, comfortable, and seasonally appropriate. I know it sounds impossible, but don't worry! Just follow these DOs and DON'Ts:

DO: Check the time. It may be hot as a Dead Romeos concert during the day, but the evenings can get chilly. So remember to dress in light layers and always have a little something extra for after sunset. (Forgot your sweater? Grab a hottie instead! ☺)

DON'T: White out. You may be tempted to cling to summer colors, but that's a seriously bad call. Even if it doesn't feel like fall, the fact remains: White is off-limits till spring (unless you're wearing your *winter* whites . . . but that's a whole season away, mmmkay?).

DO: Sandal up. Some people might think gladiators are over, but that's just because they're a little too eager to throw on their god-awful ankle boots. News flash: It's *still* not boot weather, and gladiators look great on everyone. (Well, *almost* everyone. Sincere apologies to a *certain* Snark out there!)

DON'T: Sweat it. Throw on long sleeves in the middle of a heat wave and you're asking for trouble. Translation: Sweaty pit-patches are a major NO.

Have a great weekend, everyone. I'm feeling hot just thinking about it. In a good way, natch. ☺

Shop on,
Avalon Greene

Ha! LMAO! Good call on every count. TEAM AVALON is ON!

posted by luv2gossip **on 10/4 at 9:51 a.m.**

U are 2good2B true. Reading your blog totally brightens my day. U give the best advice, too. Thank U. ☺

posted by realitease **on 10/4 at 9:59 a.m.**

I actually think boots look awesome no matter what the season. Even in the summer, if the weather's right, they can make a plain old boring outfit look majorly awesome. To be brutally honest, your column isn't nearly as fashion-forward as I would expect it to be.

posted by vogue_us_baby **on 10/4 at 10:17 a.m.**

WOO-HOO! So true about the boots. Like, OMG, what was the girl THINKING wearing those with a cheerleading outfit? That plus the weird coat and then the ripped-up tank under-neath? Scary. Wrong. LOSER!

posted by rahdeal **on 10/4 at 10:22 a.m.**

There's no "i" in "scheme" (but there is a "me")

Sunlight streamed through the bay windows of the Greenes' breakfast nook and bounced off the Spanish-tiled floor. Avalon stood at the dark granite counter, channeling every bit of her energy into furiously whisking eggs in a giant glass bowl while her dad, Martin, fried bacon at the Viking stove and her sixteen-year-old sister, Courtney, squeezed fresh orange juice at the pale wood butcher block.

"Take it easy on those poor eggs!" Constance laid her hand lightly on her daughter's arm and gave her an *I'm only kind of kidding* smile before slicing a honeydew melon for the fruit platter on the other side of the sink.

"Hey, she's just giving them a good beating like her mom does with the *bad eggs* in the courtroom!" Avalon's dad laughed at his own joke while slipping a crisp piece of bacon down into Pucci's eager mouth, sending the puppy's tail into overdrive. Avalon groaned audibly.

"And like her *father* does, too . . ." Constance called over her shoulder, tossing her perfectly styled platinum bob as she glanced lovingly at Avalon's tall, dark, and somewhat dork-some dad.

"Hello? I'm almost a lawyer too," Courtney whined louder than the juicer.

"Oh, please." Avalon rolled her eyes at her sister—a complete mini Mom, with her khaki Velvet sweats and shoulder-length white-blond hair. "You put the *mock* in 'mock trial'!"

"Avvy, be nice," Martin said, shaking his spatula and sternly knitting his bushy black eyebrows.

"Thank you, Daddy!" Courtney smiled sweetly at Martin before shooting her sister a look that was completely sugar-free.

Avalon was about to come up with another mock-trial jab when the doorbell rang.

"That must be Brianna," Constance said, straightening the hem of her ecru knit tank top.

"Thank *God*," Avalon replied. She rinsed off her hands, blotted them on a red-striped dish towel, and rushed out to the foyer.

"Hey, Bree." Avalon smiled as her friend walked through the ornately carved front door. "Brunch is almost ready."

"Wow, it smells amazing." Brianna inhaled deeply as she tossed her long black hair enthusiastically. "Bacon . . . ?"

"Yup!" Avalon grabbed Brianna's hand to lead her into the kitchen, but Brianna pulled back.

"Do you think we could talk for a sec?" Brianna asked, obviously no longer all *that* excited about food. "Like, in private?"

"Sure." Avalon nodded and made a detour onto the dark wood stairs leading up to her room.

"What's up?" Avalon asked as she sat down on the pale blue velvet cushioned stool at her antique vanity table. Not that she couldn't guess, after the mud-covered mess that had been Friday's game.

"I'm starting to feel kind of . . . um . . . *desperate*," Brianna confessed, sitting perfectly straight on the gold satin and mahogany bench at the foot of Avalon's bed. She yanked on one strap of her red racer-back tank and bounced the toes of her Nikes nervously on the plush white carpet. "I mean, the game was mortifying. Everybody was totally laughing at us—or, well . . . at *me*!"

"Oh, Bree." Avalon looked at Brianna sympathetically while twisting her long blond hair into a knot at the nape of her neck. "I know it didn't go perfectly, but—"

"Perfectly! I would've settled for 'not a humiliating disaster,'" Brianna cut Avalon off. She looked sick to her stomach. "None of the gymnasts know what they're doing, and when I try to give them direction, they don't get it . . . or they don't *want* to get it."

"Well . . ." Avalon patted one of the pink puffed sleeves on her hoodie. "It's only been a few days since we merged. Things will get better soon. Don't you think?"

"But you got it *instantly*," Brianna groaned. "You made the shift so easily. And we only have two weeks before the competition. So every day counts."

"Ah, but not everyone is a natural-born cheerleader like *me*!" Avalon tossed her head, causing her hair to come loose from its knot. She smiled to let Brianna know she was being sarcastic. Kind of. "I mean, you did tell Halley that this was a different game, right?"

"Yeah, but I actually feel like they *could* be good cheerleaders. The thing is"—Brianna lowered her voice to a whisper—"I think Halley's still trying to sabotage me!"

"Nooo," Avalon said with a frown. "She's just being immature about cheerleading in general. She's completely anti-pep."

"Tell me about it!" Brianna squeezed her eyes closed. "But it's more than that. She *hates* me. I even think she might go for captain, just to spite me."

"Well, *that* definitely isn't going to happen," Avalon insisted. She couldn't help but laugh at the thought of Halley as a cheer captain.

"I don't know." Brianna sighed. "I mean, I hope this doesn't sound totally devious, but I was wondering if you could find a way to get the gymnasts to stop following Halley? And maybe, um, make sure she doesn't get elected captain?"

"Awww, Bree . . ." Seeing her friend this upset—and this concerned about her position—almost made Avalon want to tell Halley to call the whole thing off and start acting like she cared about this competition. But if Brianna were truly a capable captain, she wouldn't crack so quickly under the pressure of difficult leadership. And *she* would be trying harder to take Halley on rather than asking Avalon to do it for her. Right?

"I feel so *weird* right now!" Brianna tried to smile, but two giant tears rolled down her alabaster cheeks instead. She quickly wiped the tears away, obviously embarrassed. "Oh, Avalon! What's happening to me?"

When she saw how much Brianna was hurting, Avalon started to choke up too. She walked over to sit next to her friend and gently rubbed her back. "Bree . . . this competition is a huge opportunity, and trying to get the new squad into fighting shape is a serious responsibility. Of *course* it's going to make you a little crazy."

"I feel beyond crazy." Brianna sobbed. "I feel *certifiable!*"

"Well, then, let me help." Avalon shook off her emotion before it became an all-out pity party. "You just have to be firm with the gymnasts. You have to show that you're the boss and that they'd better fall in line. Challenge them to be the best cheerleaders they can be—even better than *us*. Most important: Don't stoop to their level!"

"Really?" Now Bree's eyes were shining with determination instead of sadness.

Avalon felt like a powerhouse. A few weeks ago, Brianna had been inspiring *her* this way, but now Avalon had all the answers. The truth was that they both wanted the same thing: to kick butt at the competition with the right person in charge. Sure, Brianna thought *she* was that person, but she'd eventually see that Avalon was a better fit with the blended squad. As long as Halley wasn't calling the shots, Brianna would be happy the team had a strong leader. Wouldn't she?

Smooth sailing

*A*valon's brown eyes scanned the shining fleet of private yachts, each one tied to a thick wooden post along the perimeter of the San Diego Bay Club's weathered gray dock. The boats bounced up and down in the navy blue water as if they were as excited about the sunset cruise as Avalon. Tonight wasn't just the same old boat ride the Greenes and Brandons often took together. In Avalon's mind, it was a mini do-over of the ruined Friendapalooza party she and Halley had thrown last Saturday. It was a chance to celebrate everything that had gone right in the past week and the stronger-than-ever Halvalon duo.

"What a perfect evening for a boat party." Constance sighed, snuggling into Martin's arms on the bench next to her daughters. Her mocha-hued chiffon dress danced away from her ankles in the light bay breeze.

"Two boring families don't really add up to a party," Courtney sneered, kicking the heel of her strappy Arturo Chiang sandal into the dock.

"Like *you'd* know anything about parties," Avalon pointed out, tossing her high ponytail proudly.

"I know *plenty!*" Courtney shot back. "I've already been to at least a dozen sweet sixteens this year—including my own, which people are *still* talking about."

"That's because I designed the whole thing!" Avalon scoffed. A few shiny brown harbor seals sunbathing on a green buoy out in the water barked right on cue—cheering on Avalon as she told off her sister.

"Yeah, *right.*" Courtney rolled her eyes. "My party was legendary because I have, like, a hundred friends—*not* because of the flowers and tablecloths you chose."

"Easy there, me offspring!" Martin bellowed. In addition to his Jerry Seinfeld obsession, Avalon's dad had a major man-crush on Robin Williams. *Popeye* had been a baffling and painful repeat offender on the family's DVD player. "This ain'ts the time, and it ain'ts the place!" Martin added with an "uck, uck, uck, uck, uck."

"Yeah!" Avalon glared at Courtney, even though she hated agreeing with her father when he was trying—and failing—to be cool.

Why aren't parents ever as funny as they think *they are?* Avalon wondered as she adjusted her Ralph Lauren cashmere tube top and retied the pale gold cardigan casually around her shoulders. She took off her black D&G shades to look at her father, who was now, inexplicably, dancing. That was when Avalon spotted Halley heading down the dock with the Brandons. Her best friend had blended nautical chic with rocker cool in a black-and-white-striped racer-back tank, gray denim mini, and black espadrilles.

"How cute are *you*?" Avalon gushed as the families hugged their hellos.

"Oh! Thanks, Avvy!" Tyler smiled.

"Not *you*, Captain Dork." Avalon grimaced at Tyler's navy blazer, red cravat, and wrinkled khakis. But the captain's hat sitting precariously on top of his overgrown brown hair did succeed in making her laugh—with him or at him, she wasn't quite sure.

"Hey, you'd better be nice to the captain," Charles deadpanned with a quick wink at Avalon. In his standard surfer-dad V-neck sweater and faded jeans, he looked nothing like his son.

"Yeah!" Abigail batted her thick-lashed blue eyes and smiled slyly at Avalon along with her husband. "You don't want him to run the boat aground, do you?"

"No need to defend me, my most excellent parents," Tyler interjected, pulling off his hat and waving it around so that a bunch of gold anchors clinked against one another. "I can handle Avalon. It's not unusual for others to envy my stellar sense of style."

Avalon exchanged a mutual giggle and eye roll with Halley as the group headed for the yacht. They'd been on this boat for a few of their parents' parties through the years, and Halley and Avalon always set sail in the same location: downstairs, right by the drinks and appetizers the club crew carefully set out ahead of time.

"So!" Avalon smiled awkwardly once she and Halley had settled onto their favorite U-shaped white leather sofa, sipping their matching cherry-lemonade mocktails.

"So . . ." Halley smiled, kicking off her shoes and resting her bare feet on the dark wood coffee table.

"We have a *lot* to discuss." Avalon giggled, looking down at the navy rug emblazoned with a giant white anchor. She inhaled the mouthwatering smell of goat cheese tartlets and crab spring rolls that filled the stateroom, trying to decide what kind of food boy talk called for.

"Totally!" Halley laughed, plucking the maraschino cherry from the mountain of ice in her plastic tumbler and popping it into her mouth. "Where should we start?"

Avalon tugged at her ponytail, unable to look at Halley without thinking about the fact that her BFF kind of had a boyfriend now. Where did that leave Halvalon? Was Halley wishing she were with him right now, instead of here?

"Sorry again about that text," Avalon blurted. She polished off her drink in one gulp and set it down on an end table next to a bronze dolphin lamp. "I really wasn't trying to interrupt anything."

"Ohmygod, don't even worry about it!" Halley scrunched up her face and shook her dark wavy hair. "I was pretty nervous about a potential first kiss anyway, you know?"

"Totally. *So* awkward . . ." Avalon nodded sagely. Not that she'd ever been on a date, let alone had to deal with a real kiss. Her best friend was suddenly the experienced one. "But you still haven't told me all the details. I mean, if you don't want to tell me—"

"Avvy, stop it. You're my best friend! Of course I'm going to tell you everything!" A cloud suddenly eclipsed Halley's euphoric glow. "I, um . . . I asked him about Sofee."

"No way!" Avalon grabbed Halley's arm. "What did you say? What did *he* say?"

"He said he wished he'd met me first." Halley's voice was grave—sad, even—but her pale eyes were full of pride. "He said it never would have worked between them. I swear, Avalon, I think he's . . . *my soul mate.*"

OH. MY. GOD. This was huge. Avalon was thrilled for her best friend. But wasn't this all moving kind of fast? This guy had basically come out of nowhere!

"Did you make out?" Avalon was still dying for—and a little afraid of—the juicy stuff.

"No." Halley shook her head with a faraway look in her

116

eyes. "He walked me home and gave me a really sweet hug. And, um, he *did* kiss me, but—"

"Seriously?" Avalon interrupted, her heart racing. "Like for *real*?"

"No." Halley smiled. "Just a peck."

"Ohhh." Avalon breathed an inward sigh of relief. What did they *really* know about Wade, after all?

"It was perfect," Halley concluded, walking over to the bar, where she popped three goat cheese tartlets into her mouth, one after another. "I mean, if anything else had happened . . ." Halley wiped a blue cocktail napkin across her crumb-covered lips and then confessed, "That's why I think it's time to tell Sofee the truth."

"*Really?*" Avalon was relieved. After all, the pep squad would be voting on a new captain in two days, so if Halley confessed to Sofee now, they'd be able to publicly reunite in no time! If they could do that, maybe Avalon would feel less weird about Halley having a boyfriend. They could all hang out together—in *public*. "What are you gonna say?"

"I don't know yet." Halley bit into a crispy wonton. "But I need to have a clear conscience if I'm really going to go for it with Wade. So I *have* to figure out how to tell Sofee, like, *now*."

"Then let's figure it out together!" Avalon headed behind the bar, opening and closing the little wooden drawers in search of paper and a pen. She was gaining her confidence back by the minute. "I mean, I might have some serious damage control to handle with Brianna after the captain vote on Tuesday, too, you know?"

"Oh, that's *right*." Halley smacked her palm against her head in a *how could I have forgotten about you* way. "How bad do you think it'll be?"

"Not horrible," Avalon said, still searching the drawers, grateful to be talking about *her* part of the mission now. "I think she's *super-close* to realizing the job is too big for her."

"Seriously? That's awesome!" Halley cheered.

"I know. Isn't it?" Avalon smiled victoriously as she held up a yellow legal pad and a black Sharpie.

"So maybe this is going to be easier than we expected?" Halley blinked when a narrow ray of sunshine shot through a porthole and right into her eyes.

"Maybe." Avalon shrugged. "I mean, Brianna might actually *thank* me for taking over. And what can Sofee really say if you tell her Wade's . . . *your soul mate*?" As much as that thought freaked Avalon out, she knew she needed to be happy for her BFF—and for herself, given her imminent rise to the top of the pep squad pyramid.

"You're so right!" Halley squealed, grabbing the pen and paper out of Avalon's hands and throwing them back behind the bar. "Who needs to plan? Let's party!" She raced across the stateroom and started up the dark wood steps.

Avalon shook her head and laughed. She *did* want to get up on deck before the sun set completely. As she followed Halley, Avalon finally managed to reclaim her celebratory mood—no more nerves allowed. Sure, her best friend had racked up a few points in the dating department, but Avalon was about to become head cheerleader—the president of pep! When she reached the upper deck, she nearly collided with Tyler. She pulled her hair out of its ponytail, grabbed the hat off Tyler's head, and put it on her own. After all, in less than sixty hours, *Avalon* would officially be the captain—and then it would *really* be time to party!

The Style Snarks

DON'T GET DRESSED WITHOUT US!

Making the Best of a Bad Outfit

posted by halley: sunday, october 5, at 9:23 a.m.

No matter how unique you try to be with your style selections, every now and then you're forced to wear something you would never (ever) choose. Examples: Your school has a sketchy dress code (I get itchy just thinking about St. Mary's wool skirts); you have to attend an unfortunate formal affair (did you *see* the pics of a certain Snark as her aunt's overgrown—in more ways than one!—twelve-year-old flower girl last year?); or you've been forced into an after-school job (Gleeners Wieners, anybody? Eep!). The good news is, you can *always* mix things up and make sure your singular style shines through. Here are my top tips for shaking up a mandatory fashion monstrosity:

1. **Cover it.** Throw on a cute coat or knee-length sweater and keep the offensive outfit under wraps until you're able to hide behind a locker . . . or cash register . . . or ice sculpture!

2. **Complement it.** From hats and scarves to bangles and beads, little embellishments can make a big diff and show the world you're no fashion victim.

3. **Kick it.** Nothing shows off your individuality—or improves otherwise awful attire—like a fabulous pair of boots, sneaks, or sandals (just not gladiators! I'm telling you people, they are OVER with a capital O-NO).

So show those fashion dictators who's really in charge with your own signature style, and say good-bye to blending in.

Word to your closet,
Halley Brandon

COMMENTS (98)

Aw, I kind of like the Gleeners Wieners uniforms. Especially the hats! But I totally look cute in primary colors. LOL ☺ I guess on some people the outfit looks kind of lame. Whatevs.

posted by fuglybettie **on 10/5 at 9:30 a.m.**

ROTF! Great advice. So glad SMS doesn't make us wear uniforms. Can U imagine? ☺

posted by realitease **on 10/5 at 9:37 a.m.**

This wouldn't have anything to do with you being forced to wear a certain, uh, CHEERLEADING uniform, would it? ☺ Sure doesn't sound like there's much love lost between you and the pepsters—especially Avalon. (But yeah, I heard about the flower girl incident. HORRIFYING!)

posted by luv2gossip **on 10/5 at 9:59 a.m.**

Have you all checked out the latest Disease of the Day column? Margie and Olive make malaria sound mesmerizing! Click here to read all about it.

posted by dissect_this **on 10/5 at 10:08 a.m.**

Food for thought

"Sofee: Wade and I are in love. But your friendship is just as important to me. . . ."

Halley sat on the deck of the Beach Shack Café, bouncing the words around in her head and taking comfort in the smell of greasy fries and flame-grilled burgers. She put on her Fendi aviators to block out the early afternoon rays and tried to tell herself that whatever happened today would be for the best. She was ready to come clean. There was no way to deny her feelings any longer.

"Wade is *my soul mate*, but I love you just as much. . . ."

"Hey!" Sofee looked like a sun-worshipping beach goddess as she rollerbladed up the concrete boardwalk and stepped onto the weather-beaten deck. For a change from her rocker-girl look, she wasn't wearing anything black—just a green American Apparel tank and faded jean cutoffs.

Halley got up from the rustic picnic table to hug her. "You look awesome. Different . . ."

"Oh, thanks . . . I think!" Sofee grinned. "This is my La Jolla beachcomber look. Are you going to put it on your blog?"

"Ha." Halley smiled. A happy, relaxed Sofee was exactly what she needed to go through with her planned confession.

Sofee grabbed a menu from the metal stand at the edge of the table and began scanning it as she slid onto the bench opposite Halley. "I'm starving. What're you getting?"

"Probably the avocado burger," Halley replied. She'd been bodysurfing with her dad and Tyler for the past few hours and was pretty hungry herself.

"Hmmm." Sofee grimaced and wrinkled her nose.

"What?" Halley recoiled a bit. Had she said something wrong? "You don't like avocado?"

"I love it." Sofee nodded and narrowed her eyes contemplatively. "But I'm thinking about going vegan."

"Why?" Now Halley was the one wrinkling her nose. She couldn't imagine life without hamburgers. Or oysters. Or calamari. Or her dad's fried chicken.

"You know, the whole animal-cruelty thing?" Sofee shrugged her slender, deeply tanned shoulders and gave a half pout. "I'm just not sure I can do it anymore."

"Oh." Halley nodded solemnly. *But, no steak? Or cheese?* Halley shuddered.

"So . . ." Sofee set down her menu. "How's your weekend been?"

"Awesome!" Halley beamed. This was just the opening she needed. "I had the best dinner on Friday. . . ."

"Oh yeah?" Sofee raised her dark eyebrows enthusiastically. "So did I!"

"Really?" Halley felt her window of opportunity lower a bit. Sofee's story should definitely come before the Wade-bomb dropped. "Where?" she asked, leaning down to pull her Stila lip glaze out of her Marc Jacobs canvas beach bag.

"My family went to that Indian place you told me about," Sofee said. "I totally thought about you when that 112-year-old waiter explained the differences between naan, poori, and paratha for, like, ten minutes. I almost called to see if you wanted to sleep over, but we got home really late."

"Aw, too bad." A pang of guilt shot through Halley's stomach. Sofee had been thinking about her while she was having the perfect date with Sofee's *ex*. She was a horrible, devious, miserable, awful person who didn't deserve Sofee's friendship. And if Sofee *had* called, would Halley have lied about where she was?

"You've *got* to be kidding." Sofee's dark eyes narrowed as she looked past the crowd of bikini-clad girls and scruffy surfer guys enjoying their lunch on the deck.

"What?" Halley asked, turning around.

Oh no. There, walking through the rickety, wood-framed

screen door, was Wade, along with Evan Davidson and Mason Lawrence—the Dead Romeos' bass player and drummer. And they were heading right toward Halley and Sofee. *No, no, no, no, NO.*

Halley stared down at her menu and tried not to panic. Should she acknowledge Wade? She couldn't exactly pretend she didn't know him *or* the other guys, for that matter. She'd spent plenty of time with them and she was, after all, the band's publicist.

"Well, well, well . . . hello there, ladies," Mason said in his usual Casanova style as three pairs of bare legs appeared at the end of Halley and Sofee's table. "What a nice surprise." The drummer raised his left eyebrow and attempted a cocky grin. Mostly he just looked like he was about to sneeze.

"Hey, Sofee . . . hey, Halley," Wade said casually.

No. No. And no AGAIN! What if he accidentally mentioned their date? Halley sneaked a glance at Sofee to see her response to her ex-boyfriend's presence. Sofee looked happy, so Halley started to breathe again. A smile was a good sign, right?

"Hey, guys." Halley blinked a quick hello in Wade's direction, then grinned at Mason and finally settled her gaze on Evan. He was sporting a new haircut. Thank *God.* That was exactly the blandly safe conversation starter Halley needed. "Evan! *When* did you cut off your hair?"

"Oh, um . . ." Evan shuffled his black Chuck Taylor high-tops nervously and then met Halley's gaze. Wow. She'd never noticed how pretty his eyes were, probably because his dark curly hair had always been hanging in front of them. They were a sea-foam color—not quite blue and not quite green. "Yesterday."

"It looks great—much more mature." Halley wasn't kidding. He looked infinitely cooler with the new 'do.

"Thanks." Evan grinned sheepishly. "You look great too."

"Yeah, right!" Halley had to laugh. Her hair must have looked like tangled seaweed after she'd been hanging out in the ocean all morning.

"Riveting talk, guys." Mason guffawed, slapping Wade on the back so hard he stumbled into Evan.

Sofee laughed and smiled sideways at Halley.

"So, what're you guys doing here?" Sofee asked.

"We were just across the street checking out some amps and got hungry," Wade explained. Halley didn't dare look over at him again, no matter how hot he sounded. "So, here we are."

"Here you are!" Sofee's voice was bubbly—which so wasn't like her. But she did seem completely different today. Had she finally, truly realized it was best that she and Wade just be bandmates? Was Halley off the hook?

"Actually, Sofee, you should head over there when you get a chance," Wade added. "There was a really cool Fender on sale that might work for you."

"Right on." Sofee nodded. "I'll check it out. Thanks."

"No problem." There was something almost brotherly in Wade's voice when he talked to Sofee. Halley had noticed it when he talked *about* Sofee, too. "Well, we're gonna go grab a table. See you guys later?"

"Totally!" Sofee was now grinning like a vegan with a vat of tofu.

Halley finally allowed herself a quick grin at Wade before he turned to follow Evan and Mason over to an empty table on the opposite corner of the deck. She promptly looked back at Sofee, reclaiming her determination and courage. Now was the time to tell her.

"This is getting so ugly," Sofee whispered, the smile melting off her face.

"What is?" Halley asked, her friend's rapid mood swing catching her off guard.

"*Wade.*"

"Why? You guys seemed fine." No matter how hard Halley tried to ignore it, she felt the window for her intended confession closing.

"Technically, we *are* fine," Sofee insisted, drumming her dark purple nails on the tabletop. "It's just . . ." She rolled her eyes before continuing. "I asked him about Avalon, point-blank, at practice yesterday, and he said Boobzilla is *so* not his type."

"Well, that's good . . . right?" Halley started chewing on the cuticle of her left thumbnail.

"Well, yeah." Sofee nodded, picking up her nail-tapping pace. Everything about her seemed to be speeding up. "I mean, I *think* I believed him about Avalon. But I *don't* believe he just wants to focus on the music right now."

"How come?" Halley consciously pulled her thumb away from her mouth. That could only look guilty.

"The guy is *obviously* in love with *someone*. It's just not Avalon."

Halley choked back a gasp. *She knows. . . .*

Sofee threw up her hands and dropped her face onto her arms. "And I have no idea who it could be." Halley looked back down at her menu, relieved.

"But the songs he wanted to work on yesterday were full-on *awful*," Sofee continued as she began playing with the napkin holder on the table. She ripped out a napkin, tore it to shreds, and set it aside. "He even asked if we could remake that Mexican polka song—and I wish I were kidding—*La Cucaracha*. Can you believe?"

"What does that have to do with him being in love?" Halley asked, trying to hide her thrill. She prayed the waiter would come by to refill their water glasses, since she could feel her body overheating.

"The lyric was something about a dark-haired beauty being as hot as a habañero," Sofee huffed. "I mean, what is *that*?"

"Um . . . a pepper that burns like crazy?" Halley tried to

lighten the mood. She kept herself together, but she totally felt like doing back handsprings all around the deck. Wade was working on a song about *her*! Could he *be* any cuter?

Sofee, on the other hand, was starting to look as fiery as Wade with a mouthful of extraspicy salsa. She angrily knocked the wheels of her Rollerblades against the deck. "It's insane. Just wait till I find out who this girl is. She's not gonna know what hit her."

¡Ay, Chihuahua!

The celebratory fireworks going off in Halley's heart abruptly stopped. She closed her menu. Suddenly, the only thing she wanted less than a burger was to spend a moment longer at that table. No amount of rehearsal could have given her the courage to confess now. That window of opportunity hadn't just closed. It had slammed shut. Hard.

The Style Snarks

DON'T GET DRESSED WITHOUT US!

Here's the Unskinny

posted by avalon: tuesday, october 7, at 7:21 a.m.

Überthin girls have been celebrated in the fashion industry for far too long. It's time to move on! Fact: The emaciated look is totally passé. Fact: Skeletons should only be seen on Halloween. Fact: Bandeau tops and boys (especially rock stars!) prefer boobs. Still waiting for the cleavage fairy to show up? Don't despair. Here are three ways to achieve a fuller, more fabulously feminine physique, so you can fill out the cutest clothes (and catch the cutest guys!):

1. **Have a snack.** No, water and six blueberries don't count.

2. **Buy the right bra.** Hello? It's called padded. Get it.

3. **Step away from the Rollerblades.** Instead of torturing yourself with cardio every time you exercise, try lifting weights. Strong is sexy; sweating yourself into scrawniness is NOT.

That's all I've got for now. Remember: Buxom is beautiful, skinny is scary. Follow my advice, and your clothes and your crushes will thank you.

Shop on,
Avalon Greene

Who's the boss?

"Let's take it again."

Brianna's voice was weaker than the latest celebrity collection at H&M. The cheer captain's black sweat-soaked hair was matted to her head, her cheeks were as red as ripe peaches, and she had matching sweat-patches on her pale pink Nike not-so-Dri-Fit tank directly under each boob.

"Now, ladies!" Brianna bellowed after taking a long drink from her giant CHEERLEADERS DO OUR OWN STUNTS water bottle.

Once again, Avalon couldn't help but feel awful for her friend. Frustration oozed from every last one of her invisible pores, and the reason was as clear as her skin. They'd been working on this routine for the past week and the gymnasts weren't getting any better. No matter how much Avalon tried to help, Brianna just grew *more* overwhelmed and *less* competent. It was time for a change.

Brianna clapped her hands, counting off the beats as the squad ran through their dance steps, tossed aside their blue-and-gold pom-poms, and moved into the most challenging set of cheer moves. The gymnasts' footing was completely wrong and their mistakes were throwing off some of the cheerleaders. Brianna shot Avalon a look of total desperation. She had to step in.

"Hey, Bree?" Avalon called over. "Can I try something before we go on?"

"Yes . . . *please*." Brianna nodded. She looked like she might actually melt into the ground like a nonevil version of the Wicked Witch of the West, leaving only her perspiration-soaked workout wear in a puddle on the grassy field.

"Huddle up!" Avalon shouted, prompting everyone to gather around her. "Okay, cheerleaders, you guys are on fire! Gymnasts, no more excuses. We've done these tumbling passes before and won every last one of our meets. We need the same kind of energy that you put into your gymnastics routines—especially from *you*, Halley." Avalon paused to give her frenemy a menacing glare. Halley rolled her eyes right on cue. "If you're doing this to prove how much you hate me, it's not working. You're only embarrassing yourself—and that goes for the rest of you, too. This is for a competition, so let's see what you've got! And could you *please* start smiling and try to have fun? There are worse things than getting to go to a regional competition and having hot guys check you out wherever you go, right?"

Most of the girls nodded and a few squealed excitedly as Avalon broke up the circle. Even *she* felt inspired. Ahoy, Captain Avalon!

"Okay, let's move to the tumbling," Brianna called out, and everybody returned to their spots. After a series of perfectly executed passes, the gymnasts were definitely looking perkier and peppier—like actual cheerleaders. *Almost.*

Avalon knew miracles wouldn't happen immediately, but she was convinced her speech had helped. She glanced at Brianna, who was now clapping with considerably more enthusiasm as she joined the squad for the final sequence of elevators and basket tosses. Everyone was in sync as they moved to the grand finale. Avalon was at the base on one end of the super-difficult heel-stretch pyramid and Brianna was at the base on the other. As the two lightest squad members, Halley was at the top of Brianna's side and Sydney topped Avalon's half. The lifts were flawless and everybody was about to freeze in place when Avalon heard somebody scream. Then her arms shook and she watched in horror as several of the girls fell to their knees, with Halley flying straight toward the ground!

Avalon panicked and rushed over. "Are you guys okay? Is anyone hurt?"

135

Brianna lay on the ground with a leg tucked underneath her. Halley was sitting up but rubbing her shoulder, and Piggleigh was staggering around like a Pacific Beach panhandler.

"Brianna!" Coach Carlson knelt by the cheer captain. "Can you move your leg? Is anything broken?"

"Uh . . . I think I'm okay," Brianna said, taking the cheer coach's hand and allowing herself to be pulled up. She took a few tentative steps but then smiled. "I'm fine!"

"Oh, thank goodness!" Coach Carlson and the rest of the cheerleaders looked like they were going to break into a victory dance—until Coach Howe pointed out that Halley was still on the ground.

"Hal, are *you* okay?" Coach Howe asked, frantically tucking a lock of her short dark hair behind one ear and kneeling down. Avalon wanted to race over and help but stopped herself.

"Yeah." Halley nodded and rose to her feet, tossing a defiant look in Brianna's direction. "Never better."

Avalon was relieved but bewildered. Everything had been going so well. She wondered if Halley's commitment to their plan had had anything to do with the fall. She wouldn't have risked *that* much to undermine Brianna . . . would she? Avalon had to believe it was just a simple mistake. But in the midst of all the chaos, it was impossible to know what had really happened, and there wasn't time to figure it out, anyway.

They had to vote.

"All right, everyone's okay!" Coach Carlson announced, waddling toward the sidelines with Coach Howe striding lightly behind. "So, let's all move over to the bleachers for a chat."

"Are you sure you're not hurt?" Avalon whispered to Brianna, grabbing her hand with sincere concern as they sat down.

"Yeah. I mean, I guess." Brianna's breathing sounded unsteady and her face looked bruised—emotionally, luckily, not physically.

Avalon frowned, realizing how tough this vote was going to be for her friend. But if the SMS Lions were going to shine at the regional competition, a serious change was necessary. Even Brianna had to realize that, didn't she? In just a few moments, Halley would nominate Avalon and she would finally have her chance to take the squad in the right direction. Then, as soon as Halley figured things out with Wade, Halvalon could announce their reunion and everything would be perfect. Brianna might even thank her . . . eventually.

"Okay, ladies," Coach Carlson began, wisps of her frizzy orange hair blowing in the light breeze and her lobster-red forehead glistening in the late-afternoon sun. "You all know we're supposed to vote on a new captain today. *However* . . ."

". . . we just don't feel the routine is coming together," Coach Howe finished in her tiny gymnast's voice.

"So," Coach Carlson continued, hooking a thumb in the waistband of her tight white gym shorts, "we've decided to split the teams back up and withdraw ourselves from the competition."

WHAT? Avalon leaned forward and shot a furtive look at Halley. This wasn't part of the plan. She had to step in. But just as Avalon was about to launch into another inspirational speech, Brianna jumped up and yelled, "NO! Uh . . . I mean . . . please give us another chance! We just need more time. We can do this."

"Bree, we know how hard you've been working—how hard *all* of you have been working. . . ." Coach Carlson shook her head apologetically. Even the red, white, and blue teddy bear on her sleeveless sweatshirt looked sad about the news. "But we're actually worried somebody's going to get hurt. That last mistake could've caused serious injury."

Once again, Avalon worried that her and Halley's secret motives might have been to blame for the whole thing. Was it possible this was all their fault? And if it was, how could they ever forgive themselves?

"That final pyramid was my fault," Halley suddenly blurted, reading Avalon's thoughts. Their BFF-ESP was eerily awesome. "I'm really sorry. I lost focus. But don't penalize the rest of the squad for my mistake. I know we can pull this off if you'll let us try again!"

So it was *Halley's fault!* Avalon's guilt rapidly gave way to

shock and anger. Halley could have seriously hurt herself—
and now she'd ruined the squad's chances of competing!

The coaches looked at each other skeptically. Then Coach
Howe whispered something into Coach Carlson's ear.

"Okay," Coach Carlson said, hands on hips in *Ready?
Okay!* mode. "Let's try it this way. You have until Monday to
nail this routine. No more losing focus. If you don't have it
by then, we won't be voting on a new captain and we won't
be competing."

"We can do it!" Halley yelled. She looked like she might
bust out a *serious* V-for-victory pose instead of her usual
mocking one. "Right, guys?" Avalon was dumbfounded as
she watched Halley turn around, inspiring all the girls—
cheerleaders included—to whoop and holler for her.

"I *knew* she was out to get me," Brianna muttered, grabbing Avalon's arm so tightly it hurt. "What do we do now?"

"Don't worry," Avalon whispered back, wincing at Bree's
death grip. "I'll take care of it."

Mission: impossible?

"Are you sure you don't want anything to eat?" Halley asked between bites of Frosted Flakes. She couldn't believe Avalon would pass up her favorite cereal. Then again, cheer practice had been nauseatingly stressful, and while angst generally made Halley eat more, it *always* made Avalon eat less. One look at Avalon's tortured face, and Halley prepared herself for another installment of *The Woes of Drama Queen Greene*.

"I don't know how you can eat at a time like this." Avalon sighed and stretched her legs out on the long end of the Brandons' L-shaped white leather couch. She closed her eyes, inhaling and exhaling so deeply that Halley almost expected her to start chanting or something.

"Do you want to talk about it?" Halley pressed, setting her empty bowl down on the white marble fireplace next to her.

"Do I want to *talk about it*?" Avalon stood up, abandoning

the meditation she'd never been able to maintain for more than sixty seconds. She put her hands on her perfect hips like she was about to launch into a cheer—or a lecture. "*Yes*, I want to talk about it!" Avalon started pacing. "First of all . . . what were you thinking at practice today?"

"Excuse me?" Halley knew Avalon was upset about the postponed vote, but how could she be angry at her after she'd saved the cheerleaders' bloomers-covered butts? "I was *trying* to go along with our agreement!"

"But you totally botched the pyramid!" Avalon continued to march back and forth with rapidly escalating rage. "We almost lost our chance to compete. We might still lose it!"

"Well, somebody's clearly losing it." Halley couldn't resist mocking Avalon's strained tone.

"I don't think this is the time for jokes," Avalon snapped.

Wow. She was legitimately pissed.

"Um, I didn't botch the pyramid." Halley walked over to the couch to sit down next to Pucci, who was snoring in a little puddle of her own drool, oblivious to the commotion. "Your beloved captain was the one who buckled."

"What?" Avalon stopped in place like she'd hit an invisible wall. Looking stunned, she faux-swooned dizzily on the other side of Pucci. "How do you know that?"

"Because"—Halley widened her pale blue eyes for emphasis—"Piggleigh was standing next to her. Not that I hadn't already figured it was her fault."

"Then why did you sacrifice yourself to the coaches?" Avalon wrinkled up her nose the same way she did when she smelled a Pucci fart.

"Because they obviously weren't going to keep the squad together based on Brianna's weak 'we just need more time' argument," Halley explained. "I mean, hello, Captain Incompetent? We don't *have* more time!"

"But I—" Avalon started rubbing Pucci's belly frantically.

"Av!" Halley grabbed Avalon's hand for fear she would massage all the fur off their puppy. "If no one had 'fessed up, we *definitely* wouldn't have a shot at competing. And Brianna wasn't going to cop to a mistake. But since the coaches thought it was my fault—me, a gymnast who's still learning how to cheer—they were willing to give us another chance to get things right. Because it was *my* fault, not the team's fault or the supposed *captain's* fault."

"Oh." A wave of understanding finally swept across Avalon's stress-scrunched face. "I guess that makes sense."

"It makes *total* sense," Halley said, fighting the urge to roll her eyes. "This is exactly why Brianna shouldn't be leading this squad. She fell today because she was too worried about herself and the captain vote. The gymnasts know what really happened out there and they are *never* going to listen to her after that. But they'll listen to you, like today . . . before Brianna ruined everything."

"Really?" Avalon perked up. "But what happens if the coaches decide we're still not ready to compete?"

"We will be," Halley insisted. After Avalon's pep talk at practice, Halley had been as inspired to cheer as anyone—and that was something only her best friend was capable of bringing out in her. "I just think we need to modify our approach to Mission: Captain."

"And you suggest . . . *what*?" Avalon tilted her head, the corners of her mouth beginning to turn up in an amused smile.

"Well, I'm glad you asked!" Halley grinned. "It's pretty simple, really. I need to stop screwing around. We all do. I can't ignore Brianna like I have been. It's making her too crazy, and it's not helping the gymnasts step up. Instead, I need to work my butt off and make sure the gymnasts do too—for pride's sake, if nothing else."

"Halley! My genius is finally rubbing off on you!" Avalon jumped up from the couch and ran over to the fireplace, stepping up onto her favorite white marble stage. "You should use the 'outcheer the cheerleaders' motivation. That totally works."

"It does." Halley nodded. "And *you* came up with that. See? Unlike *Brianna*, you speak cheer *and* gymnast fluently—so you can be Brianna's translator when she's making no sense. Which is, like, ninety-nine percent of the time."

"Poor Bree." Avalon shook her head quasi-chidingly.

"Poor *Bree*?" Halley couldn't believe Avalon was defending her. "The girl almost killed me today! She took the whole squad down, *literally*. And there's no way I'm going to pay any attention to her attempted leadership *off* the field, either."

Avalon frowned, but then smiled. "Ooh, you should totally bail on things like putting up pep rally posters then, and when we get pissed at you, you can do one of those *awful* made-up cheers of yours in response!"

"Nice!" Halley was looking forward to *that*. "Okay, so now will you stop stressing about it? PLEASE!"

"Sorry." Avalon leaned back against the smooth surface of the fireplace and gazed across the room at Halley with an exaggerated pout. "But I totally freaked when I saw you flying at the ground like that. I was so scared you'd broken your neck or something."

"Aw, really?" Halley lay down on the couch so she could spoon with Pucci. "You were worried about me?"

Avalon nodded earnestly, making her way back to the couch, where she snuggled up next to Pucci too. "And, hello? How would I have told your *boyfriend* that the girl of his dreams had been paralyzed, unable to walk, a mere shadow of her former self, all because of *cheerleading*?"

"Yeah, um . . ." Halley blinked a few times, struggling to find the words. "I'm not really sure the whole boyfriend thing is going to happen after all."

"WHAT?" Avalon yelled so loudly that Pucci actually

woke up, standing on all fours and shaking her whole body. "I thought he was your *'soul mate'*!"

"I know, but . . ." Halley sat up and stared through the floor-to-ceiling windows of her family's living room, watching the wind shake the leaves on the little palm trees out front. She softly coaxed Pucci to lie back down.

"Tell me," Avalon urged. *"Please."*

"Okay, well, you know how I had lunch with Sofee on Sunday?" Halley began tentatively, running her fingers along the bumpy sweater material of Pucci's Free People scarf. It was one of Halley's favorites from the winter before.

"Uh-huh." Avalon's eyes glowed with anticipation.

"Well, apparently she doesn't believe Wade is really interested in you," Halley confessed. As soon as she said the words, she remembered part of the reason she'd waited so long to bring it up.

"Ex*cuse* me?" Avalon was obviously offended. If there was a way to take something personally, Avalon usually did.

"It's nothing against you . . ." Halley insisted, trying to bring the focus back to her own dilemma. "Apparently Wade's been writing a song about a dark-haired beauty and . . ."

"Ohmygod!" Avalon grabbed Halley's hand. "How adorable is he?"

"Totally adorable," Halley agreed. "Except that Sofee's ready to annihilate this mystery girl he's been singing about." Halley wasn't sure whether her heart was racing with excitement over Wade or fear of Sofee. But it was beating about three times as fast as usual. "I feel like the world's worst friend."

"Well, you're *not!*" Avalon got up abruptly and walked back to the glass coffee table in the adjoining living room. She grabbed the Frosted Flakes and ate them directly from the box. Apparently she'd progressed to determination—her hungriest emotion.

"Yes, I am." Halley groaned. "She was going to invite me to sleep over on Friday, when I was out with her ex!"

"Halley." Avalon shot a stern look at her best friend as she returned, crunching her cereal noisily. "You're the best friend a girl could ever ask for. And hello? Look how worried you are about hurting Sofee—to a kind of irrational degree, I have to say. You're *so not* doing anything wrong. You and Wade are meant to be. That's not your fault. It's . . . fate. *Destiny.*"

"But how can I expect Sofee to get that?" Halley cast her eyes up to the ceiling to search the high, exposed beams for an answer.

"You know what?" Avalon said firmly. "You just need to wait till she's, like, completely over him. Maybe until she meets someone new . . . ?"

Of course! Avalon had never been more right. Time was the only thing that healed a broken heart. *Everybody* knew that.

"Which I guess could be forever, given the tragedy that is Sofee Hughes." Avalon laughed.

"Hey . . . don't do that." Halley shook her head. "Stick with 'genius,' and leave the 'evil' out of it."

"Sorry." Avalon held the box of Frosted Flakes out to Halley as a peace offering. At the scent of food, Pucci leapt to attention. Halley grabbed a handful and fed a few to the puppy before stuffing the rest into her mouth. "So, you know what that means?" Avalon grinned.

"What?" Halley asked, not sure she wanted an answer.

"We need to take Mission: Boyfriend to the next level too!" Now Avalon was embracing the cereal box.

"Meaning?" Halley narrowed her eyes, trying not to laugh at her best friend's psycho-giddiness.

"Meaning . . . Sofee needs more proof that Wade is into me." Avalon held the box in front of her while she did a high kick.

Halley scowled and shook her head.

"What?" Avalon pouted. "You don't think I can do it?"

"It's not that—" Halley started, but Avalon cut her off again.

"Because I totally can!" She knelt down to lock eyes with Halley. "I just need to take my relationship with Wade more public—so *everybody* can see what's happening. The more witnesses we have, the more Sofee will believe it."

Hmmm, maybe . . .

"Okay." Halley felt her resistance wearing thin. "But then I *have* to tell Wade what's going on."

"WHAT?" Avalon nearly choked on a Frosted Flake. "No way!"

"Why not?" Halley frowned. She'd wanted to tell Wade about the plan from day one—but she wasn't exactly sure how to explain it. She had hoped Avalon might have some suggestions.

"Um, one, because he'll never understand." Avalon shook her head at Halley.

"Yes, he will!" Halley leapt to her almost-boyfriend's defense.

"You *seriously* think we can tell him that *I'm* pretending to like him so *you* can be alone with him so *Sofee* won't get pissed?" Avalon threw her head back and laughed. "Guys' brains don't work that way, Hal. The less they know about what's going on behind the scenes, the better. Otherwise they just get confused."

"Hmmm." Halley began to cave. Avalon knew a lot about relationships. Not because she had any real-life experience per se, but she had read every "Dating Red Flags," "Flirting Secrets," and "Guy Guide" article ever written.

"Okay. And *two*," Avalon continued, "if we tell anyone—and I do mean *anyone*—about our plan, we risk being exposed. We'll be sitting ducks. Completely vulnerable. You might as well say buh-bye, boyfriend, and we'll probably both get kicked off the pep squad for, like, treason or something."

"Ohmygod." Halley furrowed her brow and shook her head. "But Wade wouldn't tell anybody about our plan if I swore him to secrecy."

"Do you *really* know that?" Avalon demanded. "Seriously, Hal, this is my entire cheerleading future we're talking about. And I know you're madly in love with him, but you just met! Please! If you're really my best friend, you'll never tell a soul—or a *soul mate*—about any of this."

The more Halley thought about it, the more she knew her best friend was right. Looping anyone into the plan—even Wade—could be disastrous for them both. And Halley couldn't live with herself if she knew she'd done something to mess up Avalon's dreams or break the BFF bond they'd spent a lifetime building.

"So what exactly will you do?" Halley finally asked.

Avalon thought for a minute and then grinned. "I'll tell Sofee that Wade's been giving me *private* performances!" she squealed.

"Dude, she'll *kill* you!" Halley smirked, admittedly amused.

"Better me than you, right?" Avalon laughed. "Ooh! And next time I see the band together, I'll rush over and give Wade a huge hug and tell him I can't *wait* for the next show!"

"Ohmygod, and I'll totally accuse you of being a crush-stealer!" Halley said. "So Sofee will know I'm completely on her side."

"Great idea!" Avalon grinned.

"Hey, that reminds me," Halley added. "The Dead Romeos are playing this Friday after the game. I'm gonna tell the whole pep squad to go so they can see how *real* performers deal with the spotlight."

"Good idea." Avalon nodded.

Halley sighed dreamily. Ever since Sofee had told her about the show, she'd been picturing hanging out backstage with Wade—but just as quickly dismissed the idea when she realized how impossible it would be to find a Sofee-free moment.

"Okay then," Halley murmured, allowing a ray of hope to break through her clouds of doubt. "I guess it's worth a shot."

"No, it's worth *everything!*" Avalon yelled, and started rah-rah-rah-ing around the room using the Frosted Flakes box as a rectangular pom-pom. "If you really love Wade, you have to go for it. It's all or nothing!"

"Well, then, I choose all!" Halley laughed.

More than ever, Halley knew her best friend truly was meant to be a captain. She also knew—more deeply than she'd ever known anything—that Wade was meant to be her boyfriend. And with Avalon in her corner, nothing would get in the way of destiny!

The Style Snarks

DON'T GET DRESSED WITHOUT US!

What's Your Type?

posted by halley: thursday, october 9, at 7:19 a.m.

News flash to certain Snarks who are perpetually PMSing (or just act like it): Some girls are naturally thin. No matter how many pints of ice cream we eat, we still have to shop for smaller clothes than certain overendowed Boobzillas (no offense to MOST of you who've been blessed with breasts). But the truth is anyone can look cute if she knows how to accentuate the positives. So here's the REAL skinny on the best fashions for EVERY physique.

YOUR CELEB BODY TYPE: Kelly Osbourne
ALSO KNOWN AS: The apple shape
TRY ON: Stick with ONE-color outfits (monochromatic) and go with pieces like tunics, sleek pants, and accessories that draw attention to slimmer parts of the body (like your neck!).
TOSS OFF: Crazy patterns, vertical stripes, belly shirts (yikes!), short-shorts, and anything that cuts you off in

the places you need to hide the most. PS: Get rid of those heavy clogs, which just make your cute little feet look larger.

YOUR CELEB BODY TYPE: The Olsen Twins
ALSO KNOWN AS: Twizzler-thin
TRY ON: Bermuda shorts, minis, tanks, tees—anything with simple lines. Mix it up with bold patterns, prints, and colors.
TOSS OFF: Bulky sweaters and anything oversize. Sorry, M.K. and Ash, but why do you still look like a pair of toddlers borrowing Mommy's clothes?

YOUR CELEB BODY TYPE: Beyoncé
ALSO KNOWN AS: The pear shape
TRY ON: Bright, patterned sweaters, halters, and bustiers that add oomph to your top half; dark boot-leg jeans, A-line skirts, or gaucho pants that distract from all that junk in your trunk; and shoes with height, to lengthen your legs.
TOSS OFF: Tight shorts, microminis, capris, and flat shoes that make your legs look shorter and thicker, and formfitting tops that emphasize how much smaller you are upstairs.

YOUR CELEB BODY TYPE: Jessica Simpson
ALSO KNOWN AS: The hourglass
TRY ON: Statement belts, long pants, and anything that accentuates your tiny waist and shapely curves—without drawing *too* much attention.
TOSS OFF: Tube and halter tops, tight sweaters, and microminis that scream, "Please, please, please look at me!" Neediness and overexposure are *never* attractive, and definitely no way to score a cute guy.

YOUR CELEB BODY TYPE: Lindsay Lohan
ALSO KNOWN AS: An upside-down pear
TRY ON: Dark, simple V-necklines that slim down your top half with full, flirty skirts or wide-legged bottoms to balance you out.
TOSS OFF: Bulky, busy tops that make you look even more boobie-licious, with tight, formfitting bottoms that just make your barely there butt look even smaller. (Sorry, LiLo, but your look is a big NO-han!)

Oh, and JSYK: Some guys go for skinny Minnies and some prefer voluptuous vixens. So how about if we all stop giving each other body-image issues, hmmm? Size-bashing is never in style! Climbing off the soapbox now . . .

Word to your closet,
Halley Brandon

Great column, but I miss Team Halvalon. Any chance of a reconciliation? U belong 2gether! ☹

posted by realitease **on 10/9 at 7:31 a.m.**

Heard about the pyramid disaster the other day. Yikes! I would say break a leg at your next practice, but apparently the gymnasts will see to that! ☺

posted by luv2gossip **on 10/9 at 7:47 a.m.**

Big news, everyone! Tomorrow's *Daily* column will be featuring a brand-new disease of the day. Click here to read all about . . . the bubonic plague!

posted by dissect_this **on 10/9 at 7:52 a.m.**

Didn't I hear someone say all of Team Avalon has the bubonic plague? Oh, wait, no, that's the BOOB-onic plague. LOL! ☺ Awesome column, Hal.

posted by rockgirrrl **on 10/9 at 7:58 a.m.**

Bust a move

"There you are!" Brianna waved frantically as Avalon made her way toward the bank of gold lockers where all of the cheerleaders except Halley were clutching rolls of masking tape and poster tubes.

"Check this out." Brianna led Avalon down the hall with the squad following closely behind. "What's up with *that*?" she demanded, pointing to a wall of windows where Halley stood with Sofee, taping up flyers.

"How should I know?" Avalon feigned innocence and walked purposefully over to Halley. She grabbed one of the flyers out of her faux enemy's hand.

"Excuse me," Halley fumed convincingly, her blue eyes raging like a whirlpool during a tropical monsoon. "What do you think you're doing?"

"Yeah, those are the property of the Dead Romeos."

Sofee glared at Avalon with twice Halley's intensity. She yanked the flyer away from Avalon so aggressively the paper nearly ripped.

"Oh, really?" Avalon tossed her long blond hair behind her shoulders and grabbed the flyer back from Sofee. "Well, then I'm sure Wade would want me to have one. I *am* his number one fan, you know."

"Yeah, right." Sofee snorted with such agitation, the little faux-tough-girl stud in her nose looked like it might shoot right into Avalon's head. "You've hardly ever heard us play."

"Oh, I've heard plenty." Avalon placed one hand on her hip and pushed out her chest for emphasis. "Private solo performances are actually his specialty."

"Liar!" Halley spat, stomping a brown suede Seychelles boot down on SMS's gold-carpeted hallway.

Ohmygod! Halley was totally channeling the Greene dramatic flair. Avalon was so proud she almost lost her frenemy focus.

"Believe what you want," Avalon offered, getting back into character. She squared her shoulders and tugged down on the hem of the pink vintage music tee she and Halley had found boxed up in the Brandons' garage. If enduring the stench of stale mothballs for the good of their cause wasn't commitment, Avalon didn't know what was. "I'll just see you at the show tomorrow night."

"You're so not coming to see us." Sofee sounded like she

was pleading rather than telling. It was clear that, despite Sofee's earlier doubts, she still totally saw Avalon as a threat.

"I so *am*," Avalon said confidently. She marched back over to the pep squad and turned on her heel to glare at Halley again. "Oh, and Hal?"

"What?" Halley snapped.

"When you're done pretending to be a publicist with your little pierceaholic playmate, we could use your help with *these*." Avalon gently took one of the poster tubes from Brianna. "You *are* a member of this squad, after all."

"AWESOME! Rad! I'll see you in a tad!" Halley squealed in exaggerated cheer-voice, throwing in an off-balance herkie before collapsing into hysterics with Sofee.

Avalon had laughed out loud at the cheer last night, but this time she choked down her amusement. She quickly replaced it with an offended scowl.

"Ohmygosh, she's out of control." Brianna's lips were curled in disgust as she and Avalon made their way down the hall with the other cheerleaders, stopping every so often to hang a poster.

"I know." Avalon shook her head with as much discon- certed sincerity as she could muster. "I'm honestly not sure how we were ever friends."

"No kidding," Brianna said with sadness behind her dark almond eyes.

"But guess what?" Avalon smiled mischievously. "I have a plan to get her where it hurts!"

"Really?" Brianna's face suddenly brightened. "What is it?"

"Yeah, what?" Sydney chimed in, taking a poster from Brianna and holding one end with Gabby while Avalon and Brianna began taping the corners. "Somebody needs to put that girl in her place, and you're totally the person to do it!"

"Shhhh!" Gabby said softly as Piggleigh, Liza, Jocelyn Doyle, and Regina Barclay—all former gymnasts—scurried past with a poster.

"Oh, don't worry about them!" Avalon insisted. "It's no secret we're all anti-Halley . . . but I can't divulge the details of my plan yet, anyway."

"Aw, come on," Sydney begged, her little violet eyes hungry for scandal.

"Sorry, Syd." Avalon shook her head as she stuck a last piece of tape on the poster. "I can't. But trust me, it's gonna be good!"

"As in, so bad it's good?" Sydney giggled.

"Naturally!" Avalon smiled slyly as the girls made their way toward the dining hall with their last poster. That was when Avalon spotted Halley with all the Dead Romeos. She tapped Brianna's arm with a bubblegum-pink fingernail and whispered, "Can you handle that poster on your own? Phase one of my plan is about to go down!"

"Really?" Brianna whispered back conspiratorially. "Of course! Go!"

Avalon rushed over to the table where Wade, Evan, and Mason were seated across from Halley and Sofee.

"Wade!" Avalon squealed, pulling Halley's secret boyfriend out of his chair and wrapping her arms around his shoulders. "I'm *so* excited about the show tomorrow night!"

"Oh yeah? Cool!" Wade hugged Avalon back and flashed a genuine smile. "We're psyched about it too."

Just then, a group of girls at the next table wearing TEAM AVALON shirts leapt to their feet and began cheering her name.

Under normal circumstances the whole thing might have been embarrassing, but in this case it was just the extra push Avalon needed. She pulled her shoulders back to nod at her admirers and saw Wade's eyes drift down to the words SHAKESPEARE'S SISTER stretched across her chest. A quick glance over at Sofee and Halley, and it was all worth it. The only thing that could have been sweeter than the horrified look on Sofee's face just then would be winning that captain vote on Monday. And clearly, with the new-and-improved plans in place, neither Halley nor Avalon had anything left to worry about.

The big chill

*H*alley breathed in the cool night air and stared up at the moon—a perfect half circle hanging brightly in the clear, star-dotted sky. She could hear the waves crashing on the beach a few blocks away. Or maybe it was just the sound of the Houstons' dishwasher whirring in the kitchen. Either way, it was almost nine thirty and she was sitting on the steps of Wade's back porch. How much better could life get?

"Okay, here you go . . ."

Halley turned to see Wade carrying two ice-cream cones. He handed one to her.

"Oooh, thanks!" Halley knew she sounded unnaturally excited. But Wade had called her after rehearsal and practically begged her to come over. She felt like her whole life had been leading up to this night.

"Wait . . . *you* eat pistachio ice cream?" Halley took a closer look at the cone in Wade's hand. *Not possible.*

"Yup," Wade replied, sitting so close to Halley their legs touched. "And Häagen-Dazs is the pistachio master."

Halley was floored. The only person she'd ever encountered who understood the genius of Häagen-Dazs pistachio was her dad. She'd spent years trying to convince Avalon it was the only ice cream worth eating, but Avalon was a strawberry girl—and the truth was, Halley was usually glad she didn't have to share, even with her best friend. Now she couldn't imagine anything more romantic than splitting a pint with Wade. As if Halley had needed another sign that they were meant to be together.

"Hellooo?" a high-pitched voice suddenly called out from the other side of the back fence, interrupting the moment. "Anybody home?"

Wade shrugged at Halley and jumped up from the porch, stomping toward the tall, whitewashed gate. Halley seized the guy-free moment to scarf down half of her cone, unobserved. When Wade got to the fence, the motion-detector floodlights turned on, illuminating the entire backyard and the new arrivals: Evan, Mason . . . and . . . *Ohmygod,* was *Sofee* with them? Halley considered running inside to hide, but there was no time. The guys were already walking toward her. She breathed a sigh of relief when she saw this was a Sofee-free visit.

"Hey, Halley!" Mason bopped his shaggy blond head from side to side as he made his way over to the porch. "What're *you* doing here so late?" He raised and lowered his eyebrows suggestively and then winked over at Wade.

"Oh, you know, just talking about the publicity campaign for the band . . . ? The Espresso Self gig is coming up." Halley said, entirely unconvincingly. Mason had to know something was going on between her and Wade . . . right?

"Well, I refuse to do any more interviews!" Mason declared in his best diva voice. "I mean, you've got me booked solid for the next year and I feel like I'm nothing more than a product to all these journalists. And the girls! THE GIRLS! They just won't leave me ALONE!" Mason covered his face with his hands. Evan and Wade just stared at him like he was deranged.

"Dude." Evan shook his head at Mason. "You need to be medicated."

Halley and Wade exchanged an amused glance.

"So, what are *you guys* doing here?" Wade asked. He took a giant bite from his cone and shot Halley an apologetic, heart-melting look.

"We brought you something." Mason slapped Wade on the back and then pulled a CD from the inside pocket of his hooded army-green bomber jacket.

"No way!" Wade's face lit up. "The demo?" He grabbed for the CD, but Mason yanked it away and ran to the middle of the yard. Wade easily tackled him and shoved his half-eaten ice cream into the drummer's round, baby-smooth face.

"Heyyy!" Mason squealed. He sat up on the lawn and dropped the CD so he could wipe the pistachio sludge from his cheeks with the arm of his jacket. "Gross, dude!" Wade immediately plucked the disc from the grass and raced over to the hammock on the other side of the yard.

Halley looked over at Evan, who offered her a *yes, they are entirely absurd* eye roll.

"Once again proving that girls mature faster than boys . . . !" Halley smiled as Evan sat down on the step next to her.

"Hey, we don't *all* act like second-graders." Evan grinned back with quiet confidence. The new haircut was really working for him. He was like a completely different Evan from the guy Halley had seen, but never really noticed, at school all these years.

"So, are you and Wade really working on band stuff or . . . ?" Evan asked, kicking the heel of one black Chuck Taylor high-top against the front of the rickety porch step.

"Or . . . *what*?" Halley wrinkled up her lightly freckled nose and let out a giggle.

"I dunno." Evan shrugged and scratched his fingers through his dark, close-cropped curls. "It just seems like there might be something going on. . . ."

Before Evan could finish his thought, Wade and Mason stormed the deck.

"Come on, man!" Mason pulled the CD from Wade's hand. "We've gotta listen to this."

"Um . . ." Wade looked down at Halley, his dark eyes flickering between excitement and regret. "Do you mind?"

"No, not at all." Halley smiled, realizing that she wasn't invited to the listening party. She felt a little off balance after the partial-band ambush anyway. "You guys go ahead. I need to get home."

"Hey, wait. . . ." Wade gave Halley a dreamy *I don't want you to leave yet* look. He turned to Evan and Mason. "Meet me inside?"

Mason whistled as he and Evan opened the door to the gray bungalow and disappeared.

"Wow." Wade frowned. "Sorry about that."

"It's okay," Halley insisted. "I really should go."

"Hang on. . . ." Wade grabbed both Halley's hands as he sat down on the porch step, staring into her eyes seductively the entire time.

Halley shivered—partly because of the chill in the misty ocean air, partly because of the way Wade was looking at her, and partly because she couldn't shake the blinding fear she'd felt when Evan and Mason had first arrived. Wade took off his black Diesel military jacket and wrapped it around her.

"Thanks," Halley murmured, inhaling Wade's unmistakable scent—salt water, coconut, and guitar oil—which lingered in his jacket.

"Listen . . ." Wade wrapped his right arm around Halley and pulled her in tight. "The real reason I invited you over . . ."

"Besides the ice cream?" Halley giggled nervously, trying to maintain her composure while sitting so very, very close to her dream guy. Despite the romance of the moment, the sensation that raced down her spine was full-on fear. Halley could feel Sofee's presence—like she was in the yard somewhere. Was it paranoia? Or should she trust her female intuition? Plus, what if Evan and Mason were watching them? Would they tell Sofee?

"Yeah, besides the ice cream." Wade wasn't laughing. He continued to stare so deeply into Halley's eyes that she felt completely hypnotized, which made her even more worried. She needed to avoid the Wade-daze and think rationally. She blinked several times to break the spell and wriggled ever so slightly away from him.

"What's wrong?" Wade looked wounded.

"It's just . . ." Halley paused and sighed. "I'm *so* nervous right now!"

"Oh, God, I'm sorry." Wade shook his head. "I'm not trying to push anything."

"No, it's not that." Halley bit her lower lip and shivered again. "It's just . . . I mean, I think we need to be more careful about being seen together."

"What? Why?" Three thin horizontal lines appeared on Wade's forehead.

"Because!" Halley widened her eyes. "What if Sofee had been with Evan and Mason tonight? What if she'd caught us . . . *alone*?"

"What if she had?" Now Wade was the one pulling away.

"It would have been *horrible*." Halley knew she sounded Avalon-level dramatic, but she couldn't help it.

"Why?" Wade asked again, squinting beneath the yellow light of his porch. "I'm not *with* Sofee anymore. I barely was. And now I like you. End of story."

WHOA. Halley couldn't believe this was finally happening and she couldn't enjoy it at all. *So unfair!*

"Well, um . . ." Halley swallowed hard, searching for the right words. In the end, she went with brutal honesty. Soul mate–level honesty. "I like you too. But . . . Sofee's my friend. And she's upset, like, big-time. And I don't want to do anything to make it worse. And I don't know. I'm completely confused."

"*You're* confused?" All the warmth had completely disappeared from Wade's voice. "Well, that makes two of us."

"Wade—" Halley squeezed her eyes shut, trying to recall everything she'd just said. Apparently, in this situation, total honesty had been a mistake. She should have borrowed Avalon's collection of guy guides.

"No." Wade cut Halley off. "Don't say anything else." He sounded angry now. "I guess I thought this was important to you. Us."

"It is. We are. I just . . ." Halley could feel her eyes starting to sting. She didn't want to cry, but once the burning under her eyelids started, there was really no turning back. She desperately wanted to tell Wade everything. She wanted to tell him about using Avalon as a decoy in front of Sofee. And she would have spilled it all if it hadn't been for the pleading look on Avalon's face when she'd begged Halley to keep their secret. She couldn't go against her BFF promise like that. "I should go. I'll call you. . . ."

Halley sprinted from the backyard. She stuffed her arms into the sleeves of Wade's jacket and rode her bike home, tears of fear and confusion streaming down her face. The dream that had felt so close to coming true was now falling apart, and she had no idea how to put the pieces back together.

By the time she crept into her house, Halley was numb. All she wanted to do was crash in the warmth of her own bed, but she knew she wouldn't be able to sleep. She thought about calling Avalon, but she was starting to feel like a tragic Carrie Underwood song, stuck on repeat.

"YES! STEEEE-RIKE!" Tyler's voice howled through the first floor.

The sound of utter joy, the exact opposite of her current mood, drew Halley toward her brother's bedroom.

"Hey . . . Tyler?" Halley peered through the crack in the doorway.

"Yeah?" Tyler was holding his Wii remote up in the air like it was an actual bowling ball.

Along with Norm's bowling shirt and shoes, Tyler wore a black wrist-support glove on his right hand. Halley couldn't really imagine that he knew anything about nondigitally pre-programmed girls, but he *was* a guy. And he was older. And Halley was desperate.

"You got a minute?" Halley asked, walking into the room and sitting down on her big brother's silver comforter.

"Oh, uh . . . yeah. You wanna play?" Tyler turned around to face Halley. "Grab a Wiimote!"

"*No.*" Halley cringed, wondering if she should just bail. But she'd come this far. . . . "I kind of need some advice."

"Ah, troubled you are?" Tyler asked in his best Yoda voice, sitting down next to Halley while the cheesy lounge music of Wii bowling played on the HDTV. "Help, Tyler can."

Ignoring her fear of Jedi-based advice, Halley breathlessly ran through the highlights of where things were with Wade. Tyler had already met Wade, so she moved on to explaining about his dating Sofee for a few days, then breaking it off and asking Halley out.

"So what's the problem, exactly?" Tyler squinted. He had bags under his bloodshot eyes brought on by sleepless nights in the brave new world of Wii.

"I like Wade," Halley confessed, running her hand along the curved frame of Tyler's bed. "A lot. But I don't want to hurt Sofee's feelings. I don't want her to think I stole him away from her."

"Well, didn't you?" Tyler propped himself up on a classic Atari pillow.

"No." Halley shook her head. "I mean, I don't *think* so."

"Okay, honestly?" Tyler said, rubbing his eyes. "You're acting like Avalon. Guys hate games. We're not complicated. Just be honest with him and lose the drama."

"Wow. Great advice," Halley said sarcastically as she got up to leave, the familiar sting returning to her eyes.

So much for the wise older brother. Avalon had been right—guys couldn't handle "complicated."

"It *is* great advice!" Tyler called as Halley sulked out of his room.

She made her way upstairs, trying to figure out how an impromptu date with her supposed soul mate had turned into tearfully begging her clueless brother for guidance. This was definitely not part of the plan.

The Style Snarks

DON'T GET DRESSED WITHOUT US!

TGIF!

posted by avalon: friday, october 10, at 7:26 a.m.

Woo-hoo! Are you all as excited for the weekend to start as I am? Between today's pep rally and football game, both starring the awesome new cheerleading squad, and then SMS's very own Dead Romeos rocking the Espresso Self Café tonight, I've got just three words for you: OUT OF CONTROL. Looking for a little Friday fashion advice? Well, I know what I'll be wearing: my superhot new cheerleading uniform. (Go, blue and gold!) But if you aren't lucky enough to be part of the greatest squad on the planet, here's my recipe for a versatile ensemble that'll take you from the game to the gig in extreme style:

INGREDIENTS:
1 pair jeans (Seven, True Religion, Citizens—whatevs)
1 basic T-shirt (graphic tees are always hot)
1 pair wonderful wedges
1 supersoft sweater
3 amazing accessories (necklaces, bangles, earrings, clutch—just keep it to three)

DIRECTIONS:
For the game, put on jeans, T-shirt, and wedges; you'll be looking sporty-casual but still adorable. When it's time to go to the gig, add sweater and accessories and voilà! You've achieved the ultimate comfy-to-couture coup and you're looking *delicious*. ☺

Have a great weekend, everyone. See you all tonight!

Shop on,
Avalon Greene

COMMENTS (95)

OMG! Cannot wait for the game tonight! Go, mighty Lions! WOOT, WOOT, WOOT! ☺

posted by cheeriously **on 10/10 at 7:26 a.m.**

Wow, you're really pushing this rocker-girl transformation thing, aren't you? I'll give you this: THE DEAD ROMEOS ARE AWESOME!

posted by dissect_this **on 10/10 at 7:34 a.m.**

YEAH! Seaview Middle School football RULES. We will DOMINATE tonight. Be there or U SUCK!!!!!!!!!!!!!!

posted by whosurdaddy **on 10/10 at 7:46 a.m.**

Good luck at the game tonight. The new cheerleading uniforms are SUPER-CUTE. I'll be there. XOXO

posted by madameprez **on 10/10 at 7:51 a.m.**

Score!

"Is the squad on fire tonight or what?" Avalon beamed at Brianna as she straightened her sleeveless royal blue and gold SMS sweater and smoothed down her blue pleated skirt with the sparkly gold trim. It was almost time for the halftime routine, and if all went according to plan, they'd be performing it again at the regional cheer competition in just nine days.

"Completely." Brianna nodded her head enthusiastically, tucking a wisp of long dark hair behind one ear. Her cheeks were a rosy pink and she looked as giddy as Avalon felt. "Thank you so much for all your help. I'm not sure what I would've done without you."

"Aw, it was nothing." Avalon shrugged. "Anyway, now's the moment of truth. You ready?"

"Uh-huh!" Brianna smiled and then motioned for the

squad to huddle up underneath the bleachers for a last-minute pep talk. When they formed a circle, she turned to look at Avalon: "Avalon, do you want to say something?"

"Sure!" Avalon wrapped one arm around Brianna and one around Sydney. She stared into the eyes of each girl before launching into the speech she'd rehearsed a million times in her head, just in case.

"Okay, you guys, this is *it*: Our chance to show Seaview *and* half of La Jolla what a killer routine we have for the regional cheer competition. We've worked so hard this week, so let's prove to the coaches that we can do it. Just remember, though: This isn't really about them, and it isn't about the competition. It's about *us*. It's about knowing we're winners and shining like the stars we are. So let's SHINE! Got it?"

"GOT IT!" the girls yelled in unison as they broke apart, racing out from under the bleachers and back over to the sidelines.

Avalon could feel the excitement building as the girls all took their places. She shot an intense glare at Halley, who immediately turned to the gymnasts with a *you all had better outshine the cheerleaders* look. Avalon silently thanked her best friend; she deserved serious credit for getting the gymnasts to reach their potential on such a tight deadline. The new uniforms didn't hurt, either. The entire squad finally looked like a success story from *Extreme Makeover: Cheerleader Edition*.

Avalon took a deep, energizing breath as Brianna signaled for the music to start. When the first few notes of Madonna's "4 Minutes" cheer remix began pumping through the speakers, the crowd went crazy. Parents dressed in blue and gold waved giant LIONS ARE #1 foam hands in sync with the cheerleaders while the students leapt to their feet, dancing along. Avalon even saw Miss Frey swinging her glossy dark hair next to Mr. Ruiz, the cute new assistant football coach.

Avalon had never danced harder. She felt the music from her fingers to her feet, and was hitting every move as if this were the final performance of her life. She was getting so into the routine that she began cheer-flirting with random, faceless people in the stands. She was on autopilot, and it felt amazing. The audience was a blur. When the squad went into their tumbling passes, Avalon watched each girl fly through the air and stick her landing better than a lot of the summer Olympians.

All of a sudden, it was time for the final heel-stretch pyramid. Avalon battled a terrifying moment of doubt as everybody marched into position. This whole, perfect, electrifying routine could come crashing down—literally—in a matter of seconds. All she had control over was her own performance, so she tried to channel every last bit of energy into holding up her side of the formation.

Concentrate on you, she told herself. *Control only what you can.*

It felt good; it felt solid; it felt like it was working! Finally, the entire squad froze and shouted, "GO, MIGHTY LIONS!" The music stopped. Avalon let her eyes focus on the crowd and saw Wade walk up the steps of the bleachers while gazing intently in Halley's direction.

Oh, God. Avalon braced herself for the worst. What if the sight of Wade sent Halley crashing to the ground? *Focus, Halley. Focus.*

But as everybody in the bleachers leapt into a standing ovation, Avalon realized she'd underestimated her best friend. The pyramid stood strong. She wished she could see the look on Halley's face, way up in the air, watching her almost-boyfriend rooting for her. Halley must have been on top of the world. And Avalon was proud to be holding her up there.

After the squad dismounted, there were hugs all around. Avalon had to force herself to keep an icy distance from Halley, but other gymnasts and cheerleaders were celebrating like the equal teammates they were. That was when Avalon turned to see Wade heading toward the sidelines where Halley stood.

Ohmygod! Am I supposed to intervene? Avalon wondered. She didn't want to interrupt if Halley didn't want her to, and Wade looked so . . . desperate. Avalon glanced around nervously. She didn't see Sofee anywhere in the crowd.

Avalon caught Halley shooting her a frantic look a moment too late. She watched as Wade gently grabbed Halley's arm, and widened her dark eyes as Halley shook herself free and stormed under the bleachers with Wade following behind her. Halley's face looked serious in the shadow of the stands. After talking for less than a minute, Halley spun around and walked quickly over to the field.

Wade emerged looking like a dejected puppy, his eyes following Halley before he rushed out to the parking lot. Avalon whipped her head around to check on her best friend. Poor Halley! As she stood next to Piggleigh and Liza, her smile looked completely forced. What had just happened?

Avalon wished she could go comfort her. If only she'd stepped in, maybe she could have saved Halley *and* Wade from an obviously traumatic encounter. Had she completely messed up? Had she left her best friend hanging when she needed her most? Avalon knew she would have to make it up to Halley—big-time. Especially since her parents were dragging her away to her crazy aunt's latest wedding, so she wouldn't even be around for BFF time this weekened. Fortunately, after the performance the cheerleaders had just given, Avalon was confident that she could pull off another dazzling show. She tossed her shiny blond hair over her shoulder and bounded toward the locker room to get into character. Lights, camera, fauxmance!

A rock and a hard place

*H*alley walked through the doors of the Espresso Self Café and into a dimly lit room full of random hipsters with more colors than a Matisse painting in their artfully messy hair. Some of them were milling around the stage at the far corner, but most were sitting at small, round tables strewn with silver MacBooks, giant cappuccinos, and well-worn paperbacks. The place resembled an old wooden cabin, with floor-to-ceiling shelves holding a disorganized selection of books, magazines, and board games.

Usually, inhaling the rich smell of freshly ground coffee beans and listening to the gurgling sound of milk being steamed put Halley at ease. But tonight she felt self-conscious. In an effort to avoid sticking out like a blue-and-gold thumb, Halley had wrapped a knee-length, hooded cashmere cardigan over her SMS sweater-vest and skirt.

But she still felt like she was violating imaginary warnings posted all over the room: *No cheerleaders allowed. We don't want your kind!*

Kimberleigh asked Halley if she wanted a latte, and Halley shook her head.

"I'm gonna head up front," Halley explained. She pushed through a group of kids wearing assorted emo and punk concert tees, extricating herself from the cheerleaders. Just as she made it to the far corner of the café, the Dead Romeos emerged from behind a tattered purple velvet curtain and took their spots.

"Hey, everyone, we're the Dead Romeos!" Wade announced, eliciting a few encouraging cheers from the students in the crowd. Wade's dark eyes scanned the room and immediately locked with Halley's, but his gaze was vacant.

Halley quickly turned to focus on Sofee, whose face lit up with *I'm so glad you're here* appreciation. Halley struggled to share Sofee's enthusiasm, hoping against hope that Wade was either nervous or just couldn't see her past the glare of the overhead lights. That had to be it, right? She knew she'd been a little hard on him after the halftime performance, but she'd texted him as soon as the football game ended to say she was excited for the show and to talk in *private*. He had to have known that the football game was way too public a place for them to act couple-y. But that didn't mean they couldn't hang out later. . . .

"This first song's called 'What's in a Name,'" Wade said, turning around to nod at Mason. The drummer tapped out a quick beat and then the band started rocking.

Halley stopped worrying about Wade looking at her anymore. As usual, the music completely overtook him. She allowed herself to relax and lose herself in the performance. At the end of each song, Halley whistled and cheered, shooting excited looks at Sofee and Evan. She could barely see Mason sitting behind his drum kit, and she didn't trust herself not to blush if she stole even a quick glance at Wade.

I'll only distract him if I look at him, Halley tried to tell herself. *He needs to focus on his set. Tonight is about the Dead Romeos. It's not about me.*

Halley swayed to a meandering ballad. She could sense the room was as captivated as she was. Even the older customers looked up from their books, bobbing their heads along.

As Sofee let the last note of her guitar solo draw out, Wade put both hands on the microphone. "This is gonna be our last song," he announced. Mason, Evan, and Sofee walked offstage, leaving Wade to sit down at the piano. "It's called 'Confusion.'" He began to play a hypnotic melody Halley had never heard before. He started humming with a soft intensity that threatened to buckle Halley's knees. And then he sang:

"We never had a middle,
So don't tell me it's the end,
Can't we start at the beginning,
And stop trying to pretend . . ."

The lyrics were like lightning bolts of love aimed directly at Halley's heart. It was like Wade was continuing their conversation from his porch right up there onstage. He must have written the song after she'd gone home last night, and the fact that he still wanted to sing it, even after she'd blown him off at the game, had to mean he was still in love with her! He wanted to start over. He just wanted her to stop confusing him. Suddenly, Halley wondered why she'd been such a spaz, anyway. Sofee would understand . . . wouldn't she? Destiny couldn't be ignored.

The longer the song went on, the more desperately Halley wanted to talk to Wade immediately after the show. She couldn't imagine her life without him. But how could she let him know that in front of Sofee? Maybe the three of them could all sit down together and talk it through. Tonight was the night to finally come clean. If only he would look at her. If only . . .

Sealed with a kiss

"**Y**ou guys were amazing!" Avalon gushed as she raced over to the stage. When Wade gingerly jumped off the low platform, she wrapped her bare arms tightly around his shoulders. "You're, like, the hottest singer ever."

"Wow, thanks." Wade smiled down at her, his dark eyes glowing. He squinted around the room for a moment, but then focused on her and hugged her back. "It's so cool you came."

"Are you kidding?" Avalon shivered with exaggerated enthusiasm. "I wouldn't have missed this for anything."

She knew she was laying it on pretty thick, but after dropping the ball during halftime earlier, she owed Halley. Besides, the Dead Romeos were actually a decent band. Normally a weird little café wasn't exactly her scene, but Avalon was so pumped from cheering that she'd take any excuse to dance around with some of her squad mates. And she made a little game of winking at Wade every time she caught Sofee glaring at her. She was ready to drop the act and celebrate with Halley, but in order to make that happen, she had to stick to the plan.

"Well, our fans are important to us. How can I repay your loyalty?" Wade asked as a few alterna-kids from SMS walked past. They muttered a "cool show, man" and patted Wade on the back so that he stumbled even closer to Avalon.

"Oooh." Avalon grinned. "You should come to the cheer competition next weekend to root for me! And Halley, of course . . ."

"Of course." Wade smiled and murmured something Avalon didn't catch, thanks to yet another group of obnoxiously loud kids waiting to talk to the rock star. They'd just have to wait.

As Wade leaned in close, Avalon could see Halley and Sofee staring straight at her from across the café. Avalon shot a patronizing smile back at them. She couldn't get over how cute it was that Wade had come to the football game tonight to watch Halley cheer—and seeing Halley shut him down just to protect stupid Sofee had been heartbreaking. It was so obvious they were made for each other. Watching the desperation in Halley's eyes as she stood there next to her poseur friend, Avalon felt her commitment to playing her part strengthen. If she could just keep up the act a little longer, Halley would finally be able to go public with the guy of her dreams.

"Sorry . . . what did you just say?" Avalon tilted her head back and gazed up into Wade's eyes.

"I said . . . you're incredible." Wade smiled softly and then whispered right in Avalon's ear, "I wish all girls could be as open and honest as you."

Before Avalon had time to process his words, she felt his lips graze her ear and neck. *What the . . . ?* She tried to turn her look of surprise into an alluring *Wade sort of kissed me* grin. She was shocked, but a little proud of her performance. If Wade had bought it, Sofee must have, too.

Avalon looked over to the corner where Halley and Sofee had been standing, but they had disappeared. Had her performance been totally wasted on the boys over Wade's shoulder who were now smirking and making creepy eyes at her? Maybe Halley and Sofee *had* seen it and slipped out the back, so Halley could console Sofee. Either way, Halvalon's plan was unfolding perfectly. A tiny voice in Avalon's head wondered why Wade would sort of kiss her if he was so in love with her best friend, but she decided Halley must have asked Wade to play along after all. That had to be it. Worried as Avalon was about being able to trust Wade, Halley was the one with actual guy experience. And if there was one thing Avalon trusted, it was her best friend's judgment.

DON'T GET DRESSED WITHOUT US!

Wolves in Cheap Clothing

posted by halley: monday, october 13, at 7:23 a.m.

The clothes she wears are her disguise,
But soon you'll start to realize
You just can't hide from all the lies,
It's time to open up your eyes.
Can't you see?
She's a wolf in cheap clothing.
Can't you tell?
She deserves all your loathing.
Don't you know?
In the end you'll have nothing,
Because she's just posing,
A wolf in cheap clothing.
Why . . . can't . . . you . . . see . . . it?

Word to your closet,
Halley Brandon

Heard all about Avalon getting cozy with Wade on Friday. Whoa. The transformation's complete, huh? CRAZY. But not as crazy as this poem. Are you headed for therapy or what? Seems like it's time, dude.

posted by luv2gossip **on 10/13 at 7:31 a.m.**

OMG, u r so right about clothes being disguises. And a wolf in cheap clothing? Classic. Awesome post, H. You're an artist and a poet. Love it. XOXO

posted by superstyleme **on 10/13 at 7:36 a.m.**

Sounds like wolf-girl Avalon stole your crush out from under you. Or do U even like him anymore? Either way, I'm still on your side. GO, TEAM HALLEY!

posted by tuffprincess **on 10/13 at 7:43 a.m.**

U go, girl! Team Halley will crush Team Avalon! (Pun intended, cuz this whole crush-stealing thing is horrifying, whether you still liked him or not . . . you called dibs. lol.)

posted by madameprez **on 10/13 at 7:50 a.m.**

Captain hooked

"Halley? Halley? Halleyyyy!" The sound of Tyler's voice sounded faint, like he was on another planet. Which was the case sometimes, but at the moment he was actually standing in Halley's doorway.

"Yeah?" Halley asked groggily as she looked down at the orange, turquoise, and yellow circles on her bedspread. She felt like she was coming out of a coma.

"Um . . . *school*?" Tyler said, narrowing his pale blue eyes at his sister like *she* was the one from another planet.

"Oh . . . what time is it?" Halley asked, still in a fog.

"Seven . . . something," Tyler said.

"What *day* is it?" Halley rubbed her eyes as she pushed her covers aside.

"It's Monday, you doof." Tyler shook his head, turned, and left.

Monday? How had the weekend flown by in such a fog? Halley struggled to remember anything that had happened since Friday night. *Ugh. Friday night.*

Halley was no stranger to Wade-dazes. They usually left her with wobbly knees and a pleasant light-headed sensation. But this one was different. And entirely *un*pleasant. Halley's last clear memory was of Wade and Avalon, her almost-boyfriend and supposed best friend, practically making out, right in the middle of Espresso Self Café.

How could Avalon have *done* that? How could *Wade* have done that? Halley would have gone over to Avalon's house after the show and confronted her, but Avalon had skipped town with her family to attend her aunt's fourth Hollywood wedding in three years.

How convenient.

Apparently Avalon had inherited her aunt's appetite for guys. There was no way Avalon was delusional enough to think that much physical contact was part of the plan. She was supposed to *help* Halley, not use their agreement as an excuse to sluttify—unless, that is, it had actually been *Avalon's* mission to get a boyfriend.

Oh. My. God. It was too obvious for words: This had been Avalon's evil plan all along—to steal Wade by making it seem like it was Halley's idea for her to flirt with him. She'd convinced Halley they shouldn't share too much information with Wade because he wouldn't understand. She'd even gotten Halley to second-guess herself so much that she'd pushed Wade away while shoving a bubbly blond Boobzilla in his face! Of *course* he was going to try to drown his pain in Avalon's spindly bimbo arms. He, too, was a victim here, and her former BFF was the classic super-villain.

Halley had to call Wade and tell him the whole, ugly truth—even if he wound up never speaking to her again. She slowly rose to her feet and saw her cell phone blinking at her menacingly. She touched the screen and saw four missed calls—two from Sofee and two from Avalon—and one text. Against her better judgment, she read the text, from Avalon, sent on Saturday afternoon:

If you see Wade, tell him I miss him. ☺

Seriously? Halley wanted to scream or maybe cry, but she felt so numb, even her tears seemed to be frozen behind her eyes. In a dreamlike haze, she sat at her desk channeling all her pain into a bitter Style Snarks post. She thought about ditching school but realized that wouldn't solve anything. So she forced herself to get ready, grabbing the closest pair of wrinkled True Religion jeans and a clean(ish) gauzy Free People top. She pulled her thick hair up into a messy ponytail, threw on a pair of flip-flops, and slowly walked downstairs. Luckily, her snail's pace made her late enough to miss her usual ride with the Greenes.

The school day, like the weekend, passed in a blur. Halley staggered lifelessly through the halls, not making eye contact with anyone—especially Avalon. How fitting that their public enemy routine was no longer an act but all too brutally real. At lunch, she hid out in the art room with Sofee, where they silently sat working on their respective projects. Halley's wound up looking like a more tortured version of *The Scream*. Maybe it was true that heartbreak was necessary to create great art. Finally, last period ended and she made her way to the locker room.

"How's it going?" Kimberleigh asked as she stood next to Halley, changing into a green sport tank and a pair of cobalt and green striped terry-cloth shorts.

"Okay, I guess." Halley tried to smile as she tugged her lavender camisole over her head and reached for her army-green sweatshorts.

"You don't *look* okay." Kimberleigh's soft blue eyes were full of concern, which turned to mortification when Halley's face fell. "I mean, um . . . I didn't mean it like that. I just . . . you look tired."

"Oh. Yeah, I am." Normally Halley hated when people substituted "tired" for "ugly," but today she didn't have the emotional energy to care. She was all out of feelings left to hurt. She slowly closed her eyes and shrugged. The dull ache that had been pulsing in her head since Friday was beginning to intensify.

"So, today's the big day, huh?" Kimberleigh flared her nostrils excitedly. If she was trying to pull Halley out of her mood, it wasn't working.

"Huh?" Halley narrowed her eyes quizzically as she tightened the elastic on her pep squad–appropriate high ponytail.

"The final decision?" Kimberleigh cocked her head so her thick yellow braid hung heavily on her right shoulder. "You know . . . the coaches are gonna tell us if we're going to regionals or not. I bet we go! And we'll get to vote for a new captain—thanks to *me!*"

"Ohmygod, right." Halley had completely forgotten this was decision day for the cheerleaders—the day Avalon was expecting Halley to nominate her to replace Brianna. But that was before Avalon had decided that stealing her best friend's sort-of boyfriend was more important than leading the cheer squad. The only thing Halley would nominate Avalon for now was skank of the year.

Kimberleigh glanced around with a devious glint in her eyes, then leaned toward Halley and quietly announced: "I'm gonna nominate you."

"What? Why?" Halley looked down the old dark wood bench to make sure none of the other girls were paying attention. Fortunately, most of the squad had finished changing and were heading out of the locker room.

"You're the best gymnast *and* the best cheerleader," Kimberleigh said matter-of-factly. She reached into her locker, pulled out a turquoise spray bottle, and spritzed it repeatedly onto her hair so her braid glistened like polished brass. "And we need one of our own in charge."

"Oh, um . . . thanks, Kimberleigh, but please don't do that." Halley scrunched her mouth to one side and shook her head. She couldn't think of a worse fate than being captain. It was bad enough having to be on the squad at all.

"Why not?" Kimberleigh scowled.

"I just . . . I don't think it's my thing," Halley said, shoving her gym bag in her locker, giving the door a weak push, and barely clicking it closed.

"But—"

"See you out there?" Halley cut Kimberleigh off. She couldn't handle any more conversation.

"Okay . . . see you."

Halley felt kind of bad for being so short with Kimberleigh, but she had more important things to think about than the fate of the pep squad. She wandered out through the main building and onto the brick footpath that would take her to the football field. That was when the grating, nasal sound of several female voices jerked her to attention.

"Yes, she's got a super chest and Avalon is the best!"

The eight clapping hands sounded and felt like slaps against Halley's face as four Avalon Teamsters approached and chanted the words over . . . and over . . . and over. Halley squinted, trying to figure out who they were; she was almost certain she'd seen the short, dark-haired one wearing a TEAM HALLEY shirt last week. She didn't recognize the other two bouncy blondes or the stocky ginger-haired girl at all. Sixth-graders maybe? As they marched past the SMS villas along the path, their words were like a vise crushing the blood vessels in her head. When they finally got to the same spot on the path as Halley, the two Ava-clones parted just enough so Halley could slip between them. At the last moment, they slammed their shoulders into hers.

"Ouch! What was *that*?" Halley spun around, her cheeks burning with anger and humiliation. But they just kept walking and chanting.

That was *it*! First Avalon betrayed her and now her supporters were resorting to physical violence? With one uncalled-for body slam, Team Avalon had knocked Halley out of her stupor. She picked up her pace, speed-walking past the bleachers to the cheerleaders who were already warming up on the field. Halley was on a mission. She did a quick lap around the track, becoming more focused with every footfall.

"Okay, everyone!" Coach Carlson beamed from the sidelines like a proud parent, throwing her thick arm around Coach Howe's slight shoulders enthusiastically. "Gather up for a squad meeting!"

As Halley headed toward the bleachers with the rest of the girls, she felt somebody grab her upper arm. She turned to see Avalon—her eyes shining like chocolate fondue, her full lips stretched into a tight smile. Was she seriously gloating right now? Halley yanked her arm away forcefully and caught up to Kimberleigh, plunking herself down on the bleachers next to her.

"Well!" Coach Carlson's cheeks were rosier than ever. "Coach Howe and I could not be more pleased with the progress you've all made this past week."

"I'd say it's been more like a transformation than just progress!" Coach Howe quipped in her little-girl voice, folding her slender arms across her gymnast-flat chest.

"Very true, very true!" Coach Carlson nodded. "So we're thrilled to announce that you will most definitely be entering the regionals this Sunday!"

Halley exchanged an ambivalent shrug with Kimberleigh while the rest of the girls erupted into enthusiastic squeals.

"Of course, we promised you'd have the opportunity to vote on a captain for this wonderful, wonderful new squad," Coach Carlson continued once everyone had settled down. "So it's time for the nominations. Anyone?"

"I nominate Brianna!" Gabby Velasquez immediately called from halfway down the bench.

"Super!" Coach Carlson smiled. Her emerald green eyes scanned the length of the bench. "Anybody else?"

Halley could practically hear Avalon's menacing voice in

the back of her mind, willing her to stand up, to nominate Avalon. *Do it! You promised! We had an agreement!* the voice said. Halley was almost tempted to take the high road, to show Avalon that at least one of them could stick to the plan. But then she had a better idea.

"Okay," Halley whispered, giving Kimberleigh's arm a gentle squeeze. "I changed my mind."

"Really?" Kimberleigh snapped to attention, her spine going rigid as she looked at Halley with flared-nostril delight.

Halley nodded and grinned emphatically. "Go ahead."

"I nominate Halley!" Kimberleigh jumped up from the bleachers.

Halley thought she heard a gasp and glanced down the row of girls, feigning wide-eyed surprise and humility while making eye contact with nobody—especially Avalon.

"Wonderful!" Coach Carlson tucked a thumb into one of the front pockets of the tight red gym shorts encasing her substantial thighs. "Any final nominations?"

An awkward silence hung like a thick humid fog in the midafternoon heat. Halley heard somebody clear her throat. She was pretty sure it was Avalon. Then a voice almost as yappy as the mini Avalon Teamsters piped up: "I nominate Avalon!" Halley looked over to see who'd done the honors: Sydney. Well, well. Apparently Avalon didn't need Halley, after all. Maybe she never had.

"Great!" Coach Carlson smiled. "Anybody else?"

"I nominate Sydney!" Avalon said quickly. Too quickly.

Ohmygod! Avalon totally formed an alliance with Sydney! No wonder she'd felt so safe stealing Wade. She was only looking out for herself. Halley realized that the girl who'd seduced her soul mate didn't even have a soul.

"Well, great!" Coach Howe said. "It's so cool to see you all supporting each other. Any further nominations . . . ?"

After another minute of uncomfortable glances, coughs, and sniffles, Coach Carlson declared the nominations officially closed and began passing out slips of paper.

"Everybody take a moment to write down your first choice," the cheer coach explained, "and then bring your vote up to me or Coach Howe. First place will be captain; second place will be co-captain. Good luck!"

Halley's hand trembled as she wrote her own name, folded the paper, and walked it up to Coach Howe. She couldn't believe she might be *cheer captain*, but what choice did she have? There was no way she'd vote for Avalon, Brianna, *or* Sydney. Halley kept her eyes focused on the two coaches as they counted the votes and whispered excitedly to each other. Finally, they made their way back over to the bleachers.

"Well, what a close race this was!" Coach Carlson bellowed, tugging on the lower back of her white American-flag sweater-vest. "Coach Howe, would you like to make the announcement?"

Coach Howe nodded and stepped up. She cleared her throat and tucked a thin lock of short, dark hair behind her right ear, her hazel eyes squinting down at the paper in her hand and then at the girls. "Your new co-captain is . . . Brianna Cho!"

Polite applause and surprised murmurs seemed to collide in midair as Halley heard a brief but shrill cry that sounded like a dying bird. It must have been Brianna. She had been demoted—meaning the captain would be Sydney, Halley, or Avalon.

What have I gotten myself into? Halley wondered. She couldn't decide what would be worse—taking direction from Avalon or Sydney, or working alongside Brianna. Before she had time to process what might happen, Coach Howe piped up again: "And please, everybody give a big SMS cheer for your new captain . . . HALLEY BRANDON!"

No. Freaking. Way.

Halley felt herself being dragged onto the field by Kimberleigh as the rest of the squad members followed behind. They hoisted her up onto their shoulders and launched into an impromptu "Let's (clap) get (clap) a little bit Halley, H-A-L-L-E-Y!" When Halley was finally set back on solid ground, Kimberleigh threw her arms around her in a crushing embrace.

"Speech! Speech! Speech!" shouted several gymnasts *and* cheerleaders.

"Wow, you guys." Halley was breathless and shaken but finally managed to find her voice. "I'm totally honored. Thank you so much. This is so unexpected, but . . . well . . ." She thought for a moment and then remembered the acceptance speech Avalon had practiced on her. She searched her mind for the words, and suddenly they just came to her: "As much as I'm humbled by your decision to grant me this amazing opportunity—to put your faith in me and believe in my ability to lead this squad to victory—I just want you to know that I view us all as equals. In my opinion, there isn't just one captain sailing this ship. We're ALL captains, and we can ALL decide on our destination. United. Together. I hope you'll join me on this awesome trip, because I, for one, plan to head for a destination called VICTORY!"

Halley's own voice sounded foreign as she spoke. But apparently the girls ate it up like no-pudge fudge brownies at a pep squad bake sale. Halley smiled with a humble shrug as they all applauded. Even the cheerleaders appeared to be won over—except for one, that is. When Halley finally allowed herself to look over at Avalon, she saw devastation in those familiar eyes. She felt a pang of remorse, but quickly shook it off. After all, as the new cheer captain, Halley's only focus was winning. At any cost.

The Style Snarks

DON'T GET DRESSED WITHOUT US!

POLL: Fashion or Friendship?

posted by avalon: tuesday, october 14, at 7:14 a.m.

People often ask me why I'm so obsessed with clothes. Well, I'm going to answer that with a question of my own: If you had to choose between your closest confidantes or a closet full of couture, where would your loyalties lie? After running my own compare-and-contrast list, the answer seemed pretty obvious to me.* Allow me to share that list with you here:

CLOSET COUTURE	CLOSEST CONFIDANTES
The better they look, the better they make *you* look (and feel).	The better they look, the *worse* they make you look (and feel).
You can always depend on them to give you a boost and accentuate the positives when you need them most.	The moment you need them most, they're nowhere to be found.
They're the real deal, and worth every penny you pay for them.	The faker they are, the more you wind up paying.

So really, can you blame me for being obsessed with fashion's best? At the end of the day, people come and go, but fashion is *forever*.

Shop on,
Avalon Greene

* JSYK: Not ALL close confidantes fail the friendship test. Just make sure you shop around for them as carefully as your clothes! Got it?

COMMENTS (130)

U were totally robbed and should have been captain, but U know what? I will support U no matter what. I heart you times infinity and we will STILL win that competition, no matter who the (lame) captain is. XOXOXO
posted by rahdeal **on 10/14 at 7:27 a.m.**

Mmmkay, but why do you even care about being cheer captain anymore? Aren't you, like, doing the whole Dead Romeos groupie thing now? Let Halley play with her pom-poms and move on already. lol.
posted by luv2gossip **on 10/14 at 7:31 a.m.**

I don't agree at all. A good friend will always be there for you and never goes out of style. This makes me so sad. Please bring back Team Halvalon. If not for your friendship, then for the cheer competition. Divided you fall, right? Best friends are 4-EVER! I couldn't live without mine. Pleeeeeze stop fighting and make up. PLEEEEZE.

posted by realitease on 10/14 at 7:38 a.m.

OMG I feel your pain. There's nothing worse than losing an election to your BFF. You're still awesome, though. And I would kill to raid your closet sometime. SERIOUS!

posted by veepme on 10/14 at 7:46 a.m.

Can't believe I only just found this blog. Duh. Anyway, I'm totally hoping for a team halvalon reunion too. U can't win the game if you're this divided. REUNITE AND FIGHT! (Just not with each other. lolz.)

posted by fourstrikes on 10/14 at 7:58 a.m.

Fauxmance is dead

"Get over here!" Avalon's voice was full of rage. "Get over here NOW! I'm not kidding. NOW!"

Avalon raced down the shoreline after Pucci, her long blond hair flowing behind her. When she finally caught up to the puppy, she attached the hot-pink rhinestone leash to the matching collar Halley had bought for her and dragged her up toward the cliffs so they could have a heart-to-heart.

"I do *not* want you running off like that again! Do you understand me?" Avalon demanded. "Lie down! And STAY."

As she looked down at Pucci's sad brown eyes, Avalon felt a little guilty. She knew she shouldn't be taking the disaster of her life out on the best puppy on the planet. She scratched behind Pucci's golden ears apologetically and tried to process the bizarre events of the past two days.

It hardly seemed real. But the chilling truth was that Avalon had just spent three straight hours taking cheerleading direction from *Halley*. Halley, who was supposed to be her best friend. Halley, who didn't even want to be a cheerleader. Halley, who'd promised to help Avalon get elected captain. Halley, the backstabbing, self-centered poseur.

Avalon watched the sun sinking toward the ocean, swirls of pink, orange, lavender, and yellow lighting up the sky. It reminded her of one of her mom's vintage Diane von Furstenberg dresses. But even the fashion-forward sunset couldn't soothe Avalon's broken spirit. It had been in almost this exact spot, at this exact time, exactly two weeks ago, that Halley had convinced Avalon she should be captain of the cheerleading squad. The thought had barely even *occurred* to Avalon. But Halley was so insistent. That was also the day Halley had manipulated Avalon into helping *her*.

She was just using me. The moment the awful truth crossed her mind, Avalon's eyes began to burn with tears. *She was just setting me up so I'd feel like I was getting something in exchange for helping her with Wade!*

Pucci sat up at the sound of Avalon's full-on sobs and tried to lick the salty tears from her face, which made Avalon feel even worse. She didn't want her puppy to see her losing control like this! Yet the harder she tried to pull it together, the more she fell apart.

How could Halley have been so cold-blooded? Avalon

had done everything she could imagine to make sure Halley got to be with Wade. She'd even let the guy practically *kiss* her! But had Halley so much as thanked Avalon for all she'd done? Of course not. Once her mission was accomplished, she'd fallen off the face of the earth, only to reemerge long enough to crush Avalon's dreams.

When Avalon caught sight of Mr. Huggies speed-walking along the sand, she couldn't even laugh. Instead she cringed—not because his shorts looked even saggier than usual, but because she couldn't shake the visual of Halley spending the whole weekend with her little rocker-wannabe boyfriend, ignoring all of Avalon's calls while she was stuck talking to grown-ups at her aunt's beyond-tacky wedding. This was exactly what Avalon had feared: that her best friend would completely bail on her once she officially got the guy. So there it was. Halley had a boyfriend *and* was cheer captain, and Avalon had nothing left. *Nothing.*

"I have every right to be angry, right, Pucci?" Avalon leaned down and hugged the puppy, allowing her blond fur to blot away the tears. "I'm the one who's sitting here all alone. I mean . . . no offense. You're here, and you're my only real friend, Pucci . . . you're the only girl I can *really* trust."

"Hey, you . . ." A voice startled Avalon. For a second she thought Pucci was actually talking to her—except the voice was definitely male. Her misty brown eyes traveled from the black Doc Marten boots in the sand to the dark denim jeans to the brown hoodie tied around the waist to the long-sleeved white thermal shirt under an olive green KEANE: HOPES AND FEARS T-shirt to the face she *did* recognize: Wade.

"Oh, hey." Avalon wiped the tips of her fingers across her eyelids and looked back down, pretending to be fixated on one of the rhinestones in Pucci's collar. It looked like it had already gotten chipped. *Typical,* Avalon thought. *Little slacker Halley didn't do the research and purchased a cheap piece of canine crap.*

"Are you okay?" Wade sounded genuinely concerned.

How sweet. Not.

"Um, yeah, I'm fine," Avalon muttered under her breath, keeping her eyes trained on Pucci.

"Have you been crying?" His voice was soft and earnest. It was far too sincere to be believable.

"No," Avalon lied. She plastered on a smile and finally looked up to meet his gaze. "I have allergies." The last thing she wanted was for Halley's boyfriend to be in possession of the pathetic news that Avalon had been sitting on the beach with her puppy, weeping into the sand over the loss of an artificial friendship.

"Ah." Wade nodded and sat down next to Avalon—as if she'd invited him—and then ran a hand through his messy jet-black hair. Either he was dumb enough to believe her excuse or he was smart enough to let it go.

"So how's it going?" Avalon asked in her sweetest voice—

not that she really cared. He *was* the evil one's other half, after all.

"Better now." Wade picked up a handful of sand and let it sift through his fingers the same way Halley always did. *Wow.* They really were made for each other.

"Huh?" Avalon squinted at Wade, wishing she had her sunglasses to hide her red eyes.

"I've been trying to track you down for days," he said. "But I didn't have your number, and e-mail felt like a bad call. I even stopped by your house, but no one was home." Wade's eyes were so dark and his lashes were insane—way too thick for a guy's lashes. Then again, Avalon could kind of see why Halley found him attractive. He had a certain intensity about him, and those cheekbones were totally supermodelesque. More Gaultier than Ralph Lauren, but whatever.

"And you couldn't ask Halley whatever you needed to know because that would ruin the big surprise you were planning for her," Avalon said flatly.

"Surprise I was planning . . . ?" Wade looked beyond confused.

Guys.

"Look, I can't help you figure out what she likes and doesn't like," Avalon sneered, too annoyed to hide her impatience. "I thought I knew her, but I've recently realized I absolutely don't. So you'll have to figure her out on your own from here. . . ."

"Uh . . ." Wade tilted his head the same way Pucci did when she wanted Avalon to play with her. "That would be a total waste of time. That girl's impossible to figure out."

"Tell me about it." Avalon rolled her eyes.

"You, on the other hand"—Wade reached across Avalon and gave Pucci a pat—"seem a lot less complicated. And I mean that in a good way."

"Are you talking to me or the puppy?" Avalon asked with a sulk as a light breeze hit the back of her bare shoulders and she instinctively rounded her back. She was wearing a thin, formfitting pink tank top, and the cool evening air was making her ample chest more, uh, noticeable. It was one thing to put her boobs on display for dramatic effect, but quite another to let a guy she barely knew—not to mention Halley's *boyfriend*—ogle them for no reason whatsoever.

"You're funny, you know that?" Wade shook his head and laughed, shifting a little closer to Avalon so that the rough denim of his jeans touched her bare leg.

"Yeah, so I'm told." Avalon allowed herself to smile. She was tempted to move her thigh away from Wade's, but the physical contact felt kind of friendly and comforting against the breeze that was making her almost shiver.

"Are you cold?" Wade asked.

"I guess," Avalon admitted quietly.

"Here." Wade pulled the hoodie out from under his butt and wrapped it around her.

"Thanks." Avalon had to smile. No guy had ever been this nice to her before. She couldn't help but wonder where it was coming from, though. Did he think that winning her over would score him points with Halley?

"So, seriously . . ." Wade sat up straight and stared into Avalon's eyes. "I *have* been trying to track you down."

"And *seriously*," Avalon parroted back, still unsure what to make of the entire conversation, "I *don't* know what to tell you about Halley."

"I don't *want* to know about Halley!" Wade blurted. Now he was the one who sounded annoyed. But his face softened. "I want to know about . . . you."

"Me?" Avalon did a little head toss just as the wind picked up, blowing a thick lock of pale hair into her brown eyes.

"You." Wade nodded slowly and delicately pushed the hair out of Avalon's face. Then, before Avalon knew what had hit her, Wade was leaning in close and pressing his lips against hers. Unlike the almost-kiss from Friday night, this time it felt completely real. As if things weren't already complicated enough.

The Style Snarks

DON'T GET DRESSED WITHOUT US!

How to Spot a Knockoff

posted by halley: wednesday, october 15, at 7:31 a.m.

A couple weeks ago, I posted a special report on how to tell if you've been duped by artificial accessories and other phony fashions. But there's another kind of fake polluting the halls of middle schools like SMS: the Boobzilla. What are the surefire signs she's a total fraud? Here we go:

1. **She's got tanorexia.** That's right. Even when the harbor fog has been lingering for five weeks straight and you haven't seen her set foot in the sun, the Boobzilla still manages to maintain her deep, dark complexion. How does she do it? Her five-year membership card to Hang Tan, orange-colored palms, and an absence of tan lines—anywhere—ought to give you a few clues.

2. **She's a bleachaholic.** She claims she's only had her hair highlighted professionally twice. But the overnight transformation from dirty to platinum blond happened in

sixth grade. Could it be that plain brown bottle of peroxide in her bathroom isn't just for first aid?

3. **She's stuffed.** Just look at that chest! So mature beyond its years. But if it's not the work of a surgeon, what's the real story? To paraphrase a certain Snark out there: It's called padded. Get it?

There are lots of other ways to spot the sadly not-extinct Boobzilla (proficiency at backstabbing comes to mind), but those are the top three.

Oh, on an unrelated note: Perhaps you've heard there's a new captain (as in, CHEER captain) in town: ME! So I just wanted to say thanks to everyone for their support. I have every intention of leading this squad to victory, no matter what!

AND THE BIGGEST NEWS OF ALL:

The Regional Middle School Cheerleading competition is this Sunday, and I hope you'll all be there to watch us blow the other squads out of the water. WOOT WOOT!

Word to your closet,
Halley Brandon

COMMENTS (146)

Yikes! This is one krazy-mean kolumn—but I guess it's kind of true, too. Good luck with the kompetition thing and kongrats on making kaptain!

posted by kre8ivekween **on 10/15 at 7:36 a.m.**

Holy insults, cheer captain. Looks like you're in fighting shape now. ☺ Eek.

posted by superstyleme **on 10/15 at 7:38 a.m.**

Great topic! It's also a good idea to find out the surefire signs that you have necrotizing fasciitis (a.k.a. the flesh-eating virus). Learn more about this Disease of the Day here!

posted by dissect_this **on 10/15 at 7:48 a.m.**

Boobzilla. Ha. That is scary. Of course, I would never be a cheerleader either. Good luck with the competition (not!). PS: What is UP with the Disease of the Day running commentary? So lame.

posted by eternalpessimist **on 10/15 at 7:52 a.m.**

Sent: Wednesday, October 15, 7:36 a.m.
From: Halley Brandon <hallyeah@yahoo.com>
To: SMSPepSquad@yahoogroups.com
Subject: P is for Party

Hey, girls! I know I don't need to remind you that this Sunday is the competition we've all been waiting for. So let's celebrate (and sweat our butts off practicing) after this Friday's game!!!!! Ready? Okay!

WHO: The most awesome pep squad in the WORLD! (That means you!)
WHAT: Slumber party and PRACTICE!
WHEN: Friday, 10/17, 7 p.m. until Saturday, 10/18, 11 a.m.
WHERE: Casa Brandon (click here for map and directions)
WHY: . Because we rock (but we could always rock harder!)

See you all there (yes, this is MANDATORY!).

XO
Captain Hal ☺

Addicted to love

$\mathcal{H}$ alley sat at a tall white drafting table with an X-Acto knife in her hand, working on a photo-collage as the fourth-period bell rang. She wasn't in any hurry to deal with the lunchroom. Plus, she was absorbed by Mr. Von Cleese's latest assignment. So she continued cutting out the heads of blond bikini models from some German maga-zine the art teacher had provided, carefully placing them in the spiderweb she'd drawn on a large sheet of white sketch paper. Halley had decided to call the project *Tangled*.

"Hey, don't do anything illegal with that knife!" Sofee had just walked up to look at Halley's progress.

"I think the damage is already done." Halley smirked as she set down the X-Acto.

"Nice." Sofee laughed so hard she had to clutch her side when she saw all the Avalon-esque heads floating in Halley's web. Each one was attached to a spider body, with eight little legs holding knives aimed at another spider's back.

Halley grinned as she tucked a long wave of dark hair behind her ear. She felt so comfortable with Sofee that she couldn't believe she'd ever tried to deceive her. Sofee was the one person Halley could really count on. Sofee understood her passion for art in a way Avalon *never* had. No wonder Wade had fallen for both Sofee and Halley—if only briefly. They were practically the same person! So then how had *Avalon* weaseled her way in?

"So, do you wanna hang out on Friday—go to the movies or sleep over or something?" Sofee asked, raising a neon green fingernail to scratch at the little silver hoop hugging her perfectly arched left eyebrow.

"Oh . . . I can't." Halley couldn't hide the disappointment in her voice. She definitely would have preferred hanging out with Sofee over pep squad duty. "I'm actually having the, uh, cheerleaders over for practice after the game."

"Ohh, keep the X-Acto knife handy!" Sofee widened her eyes devilishly.

"Don't tempt me!" Halley had to laugh. "I'm hosting a squad slumber party." Halley cringed and stared back down at her collage. Even though she was glad to have taken something away from Avalon, talking about the gory, peppy details was painfully embarrassing.

"Ick." Sofee shook her long dark curls, freshly streaked

with green highlights—but her eyes reflected pity more than judgment.

"Yeah, but I feel like I have to step up, now that I'm captain, you know?" Even if Sofee didn't get it, Halley was determined to be the best cheer captain ever. "I mean, I couldn't exactly say no when they voted for me, right?"

"Totally." Sofee nodded. Maybe Halley hadn't given her enough credit. "So, maybe we can do something on Saturday. Or Sunday?"

Halley could feel the mortification threatening to strangle her. "Well, Saturday we'll be practicing all day. And Sunday's the competition."

"Wow. Well, it's been nice knowing you." Sofee exhaled loudly. "Sounds like you're aiming for death by cheerleading!"

"Come on, cut it out," Halley said sadly. She knew Sofee was just trying to be funny, but she felt awful turning down all her weekend invitations.

"If you insist . . ." Sofee laughed, picking up the X-Acto and slicing a few more Avalon-like heads out of the magazine on Halley's drafting table.

Halley finally giggled too.

"Actually, I was gonna ask if you wanted to come to the competition on Sunday—you know, if you're not busy?" Halley hadn't really been planning anything of the sort, but she felt like she should invite Sofee to *something*. Besides, having her friend there would make the entire exercise less painful.

"Sure!" Sofee said enthusiastically, as if Halley had just invited her to go see a Coldplay concert. "What time?"

"It's at, like, three," Halley said, grateful for her friend's support.

"Cool." Sofee nodded. "I can totally do that. I have rehearsal that morning, but we should be done by noon."

"Awesome!" Halley tried to sound chipper, but the moment Sofee mentioned rehearsal Halley's mind was flooded with those awful images of Wade and Avalon all over each other.

Halley had actively avoided discussing with Sofee what had happened. For one thing, she had clearly been as devastated by the torrid love scene as Halley. And for another, Halley didn't want to seem like she was fishing for information about Wade. Still, she was desperate to know what had been going through his head that night . . . and since. As much as she'd wanted to call him and tell him how evil Avalon really was, she couldn't bring herself to do it. She knew she'd seem like a jealous freak. A scheming freak. Or just a freak. So she'd decided to back off and wait for him to come to her. She was still waiting. And now she couldn't help but wonder if there was any hope that he still wanted her.

"How has practice been going?" Halley finally asked. That was innocent enough, right?

"Really well, actually." Sofee stared thoughtfully over at

the black bookcases overflowing with art supplies. "Everyone's been working super-hard. Especially Wade. I've never seen the guy so completely focused."

Completely focused? If he was so wrapped up in his music, then there probably wasn't time for him to be seeing anyone else, right? It wasn't much, but Halley clung to this new information. Maybe Avalon was out of the picture! Maybe Halley and Wade still had a chance. As grateful as she was to have an amazing friend like Sofee, and as wary as she was of messing that up, Halley didn't want a life full of endless, peppy cheers and hours spent drawing angry pictures. It had been only a few days, but as far as Halley could tell, a world without Wade was a world without meaning.

The Style Snarks

DON'T GET DRESSED WITHOUT US!

How to Spot a Knockoff, Revisited

posted by avalon: friday, october 16, at 7:22 a.m.

I'd hate to look tragically juvenile, like a certain Snark, by leaping on the fraud-spotting safari. But I feel it's my journalistic duty to draw attention to yet *another* kind of fake stinking up the halls of SMS. Her labels may be the real deal but she's definitely NOT. She's the ultimate impostor and the worst kind of wannabe: the poseur. How can you tell? It's simple, really:

1. **She's a clothing chameleon.** She changes her outfits as often as her mind (and her friends), blending in with everyone and everything but never truly sticking with the conformity-free singular style she professes to endorse so extremely.

2. **She's a complete liar.** She'll tell you you're a NO, but then lift your look and act like she not only improved it, she *invented* it.

3. **She's a user and an abuser.** She'll promise you one thing, but as soon as she gets what she wants, she's nowhere to be found. What does this have to do with fashion? I don't know. Sometimes life on the clothesline defies logic!

Do you think there's a fashion fraud like this in your midst? Then heed my warnings: Lock your closets! Stash those rare accessories! And above all, don't let her near your personal style! She'll steal it from you faster than you can say, GO LIONS. ☺

Shop on,
Avalon Greene

COMMENTS (164)

Wait, so is this your way of coming out of the closet as a poseur? Cause YOU sorta seem to be changing your style every other second. On the one hand I'd say awesome, it's always good to reinvent yourself, but only if it's for real and you're not just trying to be something you're not. I'm just saying . . .

posted by vogue_us_baby **on 10/16 at 7:29 a.m.**

OMG! It's like you've been hanging out with my "friends" lately. You know, the ones who ask to borrow something from your closet and then when everyone compliments them on it they act like they discovered it themselves? SO annoying. (But I gotta say, Halley's column the other day was way harsher. I think she wins this round! ☺)

posted by superstyleme **on 10/16 at 7:30 a.m.**

Don't worry, Av. No matter who steals your style, you're the originator and the one who wears it best. And can I just add that trying to rock a cheerleading uniform isn't easy (as we've seen with some of the newer squad members!). Hello? I realize some of them can't help being tiny, but the skeletonian look just doesn't do those sweaters justice, you know? XOXO

posted by cheeriously **on 10/16 at 7:32 a.m.**

Awesome points, as always. It's soooooo hard being a trendsetter when people are constantly trying to rip off your personal style. Suddenly you look totally lame for wearing what everyone else is, even though you got there first! (But I still want to raid your closet sometime . . . LOLZ! ☺)

posted by veepme **on 10/16 at 7:35 a.m.**

The strife of the party

*A*valon felt a tight, burning sensation in her chest. She closed her eyes, trying to catch her breath. When she opened them, little spots of light were dancing in front of her eyes. She reached out, dizzily searching for something to steady herself. Finally, she found a small, sweaty arm.

"Hey, are you okay?" the owner of the lifesaving limb inquired. It was Sydney.

"Oh yeah, I'm fine." Avalon squinted through the thin film of early evening mist and started to breathe more easily. "I'm just getting tired."

"No kidding." Sydney sniffed. Avalon could see her pale pink Juicy sweats coming into sharper focus, then her violet eyes and then, finally, her blond bob. "Halley's being a little hard-core, don't you think?"

"Yeah, just a little." Avalon rolled her eyes.

It was the understatement of the year. The pep squad had been practicing in the Brandons' backyard for the past two hours, and Avalon had never seen Halley so fired up about anything, especially *cheerleading*. It was bizarre. Worse still, it seemed that the cheerleaders and gymnasts alike were thriving under Halley's direction.

"Hey, Hal, can you show us how to do that one tumbling combination again?" Tanya asked enthusiastically. "How do you get so much height on the back handsprings?"

"Ohmygod, Halley's the total *queen* of the handspring!" Piggleigh flared her nostrils. The girl needed to come up with a new facial expression.

"You really are, Halley," Andi chimed in. "Like, seriously awesome." Andi's dark curls bounced, and Avalon could imagine the little droplets of saliva shooting through her horselike teeth when she said "ssseriousssly" and "awessssome."

Avalon was experiencing a decidedly unpleasant déjà vu—a flashback to the slumber party she'd hosted last month, before the gymnastics-cheerleading merger, when Halley had crashed the party and outtumbled Avalon in front of her entire squad. Avalon wasn't sure how much more of this hooray-for-Halley stuff she could take, and she definitely didn't want to relive that moment again.

Unfortunately, Halley actually seemed to be enjoying her new position. Worse still, after a few tearful conversations with Avalon, Brianna seemed to have accepted—even embraced—being demoted to Halley's second in command. Didn't these people realize Avalon was better at tumbling *and* cheering than Halley? Didn't they realize Avalon should have been the one leading the team to victory?

"Okay, okay." Halley feigned humility as she wiped her hands on her maroon yoga pants and walked a few paces toward her creepy old stone playhouse. "I'll show you guys one more time, but then we should probably call it a night. I think we've got the routine nailed."

Avalon and Sydney exchanged a mutually irritated head shake with each other as Halley took a running start and then threw down the round-off, back-handsprings, back-tuck combo as requested. A few of the girls squealed and whooped when Halley came dangerously close to colliding with them. Avalon widened her eyes in horror. *Hello? What kind of captain nearly takes out half her squad in the middle of a tumbling pass?*

When Halley stuck the landing and the girls went wild, Avalon felt the heat rising to her cheeks.

"And that's how it's done!" Halley actually took a bow.

Freak.

"Anyway . . . are you guys ready to head inside?" Halley asked, straightening her tight white camisole. "I'm getting tired."

"Hey, Hal?" Sydney said as she twirled a lock of golden

hair around her index finger with a mischievous look in her eyes.

"What's up?" Halley looked directly at Sydney, obviously not wanting to move her gaze an inch closer to Avalon. It was one of her most immature maneuvers.

"Won't it be pretty crowded for the whole squad to sleep at your place?" Sydney's voice sounded sweet and innocent, but Avalon had a feeling her motives were darker.

"Oh no . . . we've got a ton of room," Halley insisted. Avalon noticed her right eye twitching slightly—a telltale sign that her confidence was just an act.

"Yeah, but still," Sydney continued, "wouldn't it be more comfortable if half of us stayed at Avalon's—like the *cheer* half?"

Ha. Avalon was so glad she had Sydney on her side. The former co-captain was turning out to be one of the best friends Avalon could have hoped for. Sydney had even nominated *Avalon* for captain—totally risking her relationship with Brianna and increasing the odds of losing her co-captain spot. Which was exactly what happened. The only reason Halley had won the captain spot was that the original cheerleaders' votes had been split between three of their own.

"Um, we're *all* cheerleaders now," Halley snapped, paraphrasing the words Brianna had uttered a few weeks ago when her leadership had first been questioned. "*I'm* the captain, *I'm* hosting this party, and everything's set for sleeping in *my* living room."

Whoa. Déjà vu again. Halley hadn't whined this much since Avalon had been served the first piece of cake at Halley's fifth birthday party. She was used to getting everything she wanted. Even more pathetic, Halley was whimpering over something she didn't really want, let alone deserve. Avalon knew she had to say something. She just had to word it carefully. She didn't want to come across as a spoiled toddler too.

"Don't take it personally, Hal," Avalon finally proclaimed evenly, lacing her words with forced concern. It was the first time she'd spoken to Halley directly in a week. "It *would* be more comfortable. I mean, we have enough beds and couches to sleep ten each—and we do need to be well rested to do our best on Sunday."

"Avalon has a point." Brianna nodded before Halley could respond.

Hello, loyal cheerleader friend number two! Maybe Avalon was wrong about Brianna accepting Halley as captain. Maybe Brianna was just doing what she thought the team needed from her.

"Fine." Halley relented. "Go get some sleep and we'll reconvene in the morning." Then she spun on her white Nikes to lead the former gymnasts into her house.

Suddenly, Avalon felt like she could go for another

225

two-hour practice. She guided the cheerleaders through the gate separating her backyard from Halley's. At least she still had her *real* friends—Brianna, Sydney, and the rest of the cheerleaders—on her side. Between them and her kind-of-sort-of new love interest, Avalon was certain that Halley's reign at the top would be as short-lived as their faux reconciliation.

The
Style
Snarks

DON'T GET DRESSED WITHOUT US!

In It to Win It

posted by halley: sunday, october 19, at 8:32 a.m.

Well, people, the big day is here! The SMS pep squad will be competing at the Regional Middle School Cheerleading competition this afternoon! I don't want to jinx anything, but I'm fully expecting us to put the rest of the squads to shame. Part of the reason we're so awesome? We look like the winners we are. When we decided go for the gold, we didn't just work our butts off—we got new uniforms to display our extreme competitive edge. This brings me to an important point: If YOU want whatever you've set your sights on, you've got to ignore the underminers and dress for success too. Here's how to go, fight, WIN:

1. **Wear what you love.** Whether it's a to-die-for tank top or your fave pair of boots, you have to like it for everyone else to.

2. **Invest in yourself.** Go ahead and spend a tiny bit more on something that kicks your look up a notch—even if it's just

a small accessory. Better yet, look for a vintage piece of couture at a secondhand store or borrow something from Mommy dearest (if she's a fashion icon like mine!). Nothing says, "I'm the best," like a big-ticket item.

3. **Never let 'em see you sweat.** No matter what you're wearing, you'll always look like a winner if you feel like one on the inside. Confidence is the key to vic-to-ry!

Word to your closet,
Halley Brandon

COMMENTS (165)

LOVIN' this column! Great suggestions. U will win the competition fo sho.
posted by slave2fashun **on 10/19 at 8:39 a.m.**

Can't wait to see what happens at the competition today—and not just between the squads. I'm hearing the real fight will be going down on the sidelines between two former friends called HALVALON. Things are definitely heating up!
posted by luv2gossip **on 10/19 at 8:41 a.m.**

I really hope you guys manage to unite and kick butt at the competition today. I'm rooting for you.
posted by fourstrikes **on 10/19 at 8:44 a.m.**

U will always be a winner in my book. GO, TEAM HALLEY! Wooooooooo. ☺

posted by rockgirrrl **on 10/19 at 8:48 a.m.**

Courage under fire

"*L*ook out!" shrieked a female voice.

Halley leapt out of the way as three girls in red sweaters emblazoned with pink VMS letters came flipping and tumbling toward her. They were from Valentine Middle School—hence the uniform colors.

"Um, how about keeping your stunts on the mat?" Halley snapped. She followed the harsh words with a big, cheertastic smile, realizing her response wasn't exactly captainesque.

"You'll be fine . . . you'll be fine . . . Mommy's here," a woman with the biggest blond hair Halley had ever seen cooed as an equally large-coiffed girl groaned in pain. She was lying on a stretcher, and two emergency medical technicians were carrying her to the injury center set up in the corner of the gym.

The competition hasn't even started and there are already casualties?

The SMS squad wasn't up yet, but Halley was convinced she was going to throw up. She couldn't figure out why, though. Aside from all the short skirts and bare midriffs, the scene was pretty familiar. Halley had been in the Mesa College performance space for several gymnastics meets. She was all too familiar with the potpourri-bleach scent wafting off the scuffed pale wood floors, the plastic yellow folding seats that screeched when somebody in the stands shifted at just the wrong time. She'd rocked plenty of routines on the same forest green floor mats, and she'd never once been worried about any of those performances. So why was she letting a cheer competition turn her stomach?

As the members of Torrey Pines Middle School raced onto the floor in their skimpy tiger-striped halter tops and matching black-and-orange lamé skirts, Halley felt another wave of nausea rip through her. She wasn't sure if it was because the squad was doing their routine to the Pussycat Dolls' gross-out anthem "When I Grow Up," because of their skanko-rific uniforms, or because her own performance was inching closer.

Halley looked up in the stands, searching for a friendly face. Sofee was sitting in the very last row. She widened her eyes with a twinge of sarcastic enthusiasm and waved a GO, LIONS flag at Halley when their eyes met. Halley grinned at her friend. If anybody could help her take this whole thing less seriously, it was Sofee.

But then Halley turned around to look at her squad. Kimberleigh was gyrating her hips to the Pussycat Dolls. When she saw Halley watching, she stopped and flared her nostrils excitedly. Not the image Halley needed right now. She stole a glance over at Avalon and Sydney, who were perfecting each other's ponytails, and felt a pang of envy. If only Halley could ask for her ex–best friend's help. Avalon would've had a bullet-pointed plan for dealing with the stress of being captain. Of course, it probably would have included devious, underhanded things like sabotaging the other teams' uniforms.

The gnawing nausea in Halley's stomach intensified. She searched the stands again. Was there any chance Wade might actually show up? Halley just couldn't shake the desperate hope that she and Wade would eventually be together, one way or another.

Halley caught sight of Tyler scooting into a yellow folding chair alongside their parents. Looking at her dad and mom, so perfect for each other, such soul mates, Halley began to realize she wasn't feeling sick about the competition at all. She was lovesick! It didn't matter that she was the cheer captain. It didn't matter whether or not she led the team to victory. None of it would mean anything if she didn't have Wade beside her. She *had* to find a way to work it all out. She'd just act less like Drama Queen Greene about everything—with both Wade *and* Sofee, just like Tyler had suggested. Halley finally knew what she needed to do.

"Um, I'll be right back!" she said to nobody in particular as she raced through a pair of heavy metal doors into the locker room. Halley rummaged through her gym bag, finally found her cell phone, and, with a trembling index finger, speed-dialed Wade.

"Hey!" Oh, how she'd missed that voice. "This is Wade. You know what to do. So do it." *BEEEEP.*

Halley hesitated for a moment, about to hang up, defeated. But she couldn't let it go that easily. She needed to fight for what she wanted. She couldn't let Avalon drag Wade into a relationship without letting him know how she really felt.

"Hey, Wade . . . it's me, Hal." She smiled, realizing her voice sounded more solid than she'd expected. "Look, I'm sorry I've been so weird about everything. But would you come to the cheer competition? Sofee's here and I really need your support too. I mean, I *want* you here. I mean, um, I don't just want you here. I WANT TO BE WITH YOU, *period.*"

Ohmygod! Did I really just say all that? Halley pressed the end button on her phone, tossed it back into her bag, and returned to the gym floor, where the Pussycat Dolls were still going strong (although the Torrey Pines Tigers looked pretty weak). Halley let out a calming breath and then inhaled a victorious one. She'd finally told Wade that she was willing to be with him in public, no matter who saw them—even Sofee. And that was definitely something worth cheering about. Wasn't it?

The pill of victory

*A*valon tried not to rock along to Torrey Pines Middle School's routine, but she couldn't resist. They were good. Like, *really* good. Why hadn't the SMS squad come up with those moves, and why had they decided to go with Madonna? Even with Justin Timberlake in the mix, Madonna was . . . old.

Why? Because *Halley* was the captain, and she didn't pay attention to competitive details like that! Of course, the TPMS uniforms—if you could even call them that—were another story.

Hello? Skanks and the City *anyone? Just because you're dancing to the Pussycat Dolls doesn't mean you need to dress like them. Ick.*

Focusing all her energy on the gruesome uniforms, Avalon tried to convince herself that her Lions would blow these

Tigers out of the water. Then one of the Tigers fell right on her orange-and-black butt, and any fears Avalon had melted away completely. SMS was so going to win this thing! They would then head to San Francisco for the state competition (and lots of awesome shopping), win that, and then go to nationals. They would go down in history—possibly even be written up in Wikipedia—as the best squad in America.

Now Avalon's mind was going into full-on fantasy overload: Maybe the SMS squad would get a giant profile in *American Cheerleader* magazine! Maybe they'd even inspire a new *People* magazine feature—"The 20 Hottest People Under 20"—with one slot for each member of the squad! Of course, Avalon instantly thought with a sulky frown, Halley would get the cover, since she was the captain, leaving Avalon looking like a pathetic, invisible nobody.

Avalon scowled and looked over at her squad, hoping for a reassuring glance that would help her snap back into the right headspace. She even wondered if quickly locking eyes with Halley, here in the same gym where they'd won so many meets together, might help her confidence. But Halley was nowhere to be found.

Was that any way to lead the squad to victory? The captain not even watching their rivals perform? Avalon closed her eyes and shook her head. Not that she was surprised. It was so typical of Halley to skate through, totally disorganized, oblivious to all the important details—no matter what she claimed in her beyond-lame Style Snarks columns. She *so* didn't deserve to be captain.

Just at that moment, Halley returned to grace the squad with her presence. She was back with the same smug look she'd had on her face for the past week.

How nice of you to join us, oh, captain, my captain.

Avalon winced at her own negativity. She had to shake off this attitude. They were up next, and she needed to rock the floor. Not for Halley, but for Brianna, Sydney, and all the rest of the cheerleaders, not to mention for *herself*.

As the crowd's cheering died down for the Torrey Pines Tigers and the girls raced off the gym floor, the announcer's voice bellowed through the loudspeakers: "And now, please welcome the final squad of the day: the Seaview Middle School Lions!"

The crowd went wild. It seemed like every last person in the stands leapt out of their screeching folding chairs, clapping and hollering and waving their flags. Avalon clutched her pom-poms and raced out onto the floor with the rest of her squad. But as she stood in position, her head bowed, her pulse started racing in her ears.

She closed her eyes and waited for the music to start. The beat always took her into the performance zone. Finally, the crowd quieted down. But when "4 Minutes" began to echo through the gymnasium, they all shot back to their feet. This was *it*. Avalon could feel the music powering her through the routine. She'd never performed her cheer moves with such precision, danced with such grace, or gotten her cheer-voice to sound quite so husky. She cheered like every last pair of eyes out there was focused completely on her. She was the hottest member of the squad, the one to watch.

Avalon tossed her pom-poms aside as she moved into the tumbling section, waiting for each girl to take her turn. Finally, Avalon was up. She took a deep breath and shivered with excitement as she headed into her round off and two back handsprings. Flipping on pure adrenaline, she threw in a brand-new skill at the last second, going for a layout with a half twist, ending with a back tuck and sticking her landing. The crowd went *insane*. She really *was* the star!

Avalon moved through the elevators, barely able to contain herself as the squad headed into the grand finale. Within seconds, the girls stuck the pyramid, shouting, "GO, MIGHTY LIONS!" louder than they'd ever shouted before. The music stopped. In the brief moment of silence that followed, Avalon wondered if something horrible had happened—was Sydney dangling upside down above her? But then the crowd erupted in screams and applause. All for the SMS squad! All for AVALON!

"You did it!" Coach Carlson bellowed as she stood in one corner of the gym, welcoming the girls with open arms as they all jogged over.

"You were phenomenal!" Coach Howe chimed in, throwing her tiny-but-muscular arms around Halley and Brianna.

Avalon's heart plummeted. Hadn't they *all* been phenomenal? Why was the gymnastics coach giving all her attention to Halley and Brianna, emphasis on *Halley*? Avalon felt invisible once again. She tried to talk herself down before she slipped into a jealous rage. She wanted to stay positive while they waited for the results. That was all that mattered, right? The win?

After what felt like hours, the judges finally filed out to a folding table in the middle of the gym floor, where two small trophies flanked a giant one. Avalon barely gave the little trophies a second glance. They had rocked the competition. Nobody else could touch them. How could it go any other way?

Avalon stood between Brianna and Sydney. She could feel her two closest friends trembling right along with her. She glanced over at Halley, who was clutching Piggleigh's and Liza's hands.

Some captain, Avalon thought as Torrey Pines took home the second-runner-up trophy. Even though the SMS squad looked like a united team, in reality they were as divided as ever, the cheerleaders huddled separate from the gymnasts.

"And the winner of the regional competition is . . . the SEAVIEW MIDDLE SCHOOL LIONS!"

She *knew* it! Avalon hugged Brianna and Sydney close.

They all got swept up in a mass of bodies as the squad raced out to join the judges. At gymnastics meets, the entire team would lift up the trophy together, so Avalon reached out to put her hand on the gold-and-metallic-blue prize. Halley swatted Avalon's hand out of the way, reaching to grasp one side of the trophy and allowing Brianna to hold the other side as they raised it up over their heads. Avalon recoiled in horror and humiliation.

Despite the cheers filling the gym, Avalon was utterly defeated. She'd lost. There was no way that all eyes were on her now. Actually, there probably weren't *any* eyes on her. She blinked furiously to hold back her tears and glanced over at Halley—the *pep fraud*, who looked absurdly pleased with herself. As if any of this would have been possible without Avalon. Somebody needed to wipe that smug look off her face. As she wrapped one arm around Sydney and another around Andi and looked to the stands, Avalon realized that wouldn't be so hard after all.

The agony of defeat

*H*alley was walking on billowy, fluffy clouds of euphoric bliss. She didn't feel nauseated anymore. Her parents had invited the entire squad over for a celebratory barbecue, and her stomach was rumbling for some of her dad's famous organic turkey burgers. She was ready for a victory dinner! She had led the squad to first place! She couldn't wait to share the news with Wade and move on to completing her next mission: becoming the cutest couple on campus. Maybe she'd even invite him to the barbecue.

Halley walked down the concrete steps in front of the gym with her parents, Tyler, and a few of her squad mates, inhaling the scent of warm grass and searching for Sofee. Crowds of people milled around, some congratulating one another and others consoling the trophyless squads. That was when she saw him, standing in the middle of the green

241

field by an imposing stone basketball statue, the sun illuminating his flawless features: WADE!

"Ohmygod!" Halley squealed and dropped her gym bag, picking up the pace as she headed toward him. She couldn't have planned a more perfect end to this day. He'd come to see her. To celebrate with her!

Wade's face brightened and a halo of light seemed to encircle his messy black hair as he looked in Halley's direction. It was like one of those slow-motion love scenes from the movies where everything got all fuzzy as they got closer and closer. Then, just when things felt like they were going to flip back to real speed, the scene came to a screeching halt. Someone brushed past Halley and leapt directly into Wade's arms.

AVALON?

Halley froze in place as she watched Wade wrap his arms around the girl she'd once called her best friend. He lifted Avalon up and hugged her tight, then kissed her blissfully. Sure, it was only on the cheek, but it looked way more meaningful than the peck he'd given Halley after their date. Halley desperately wanted to look somewhere else, but it was like seeing a woman who'd mistaken tights for leggings and ended up walking around overly exposed in public. She was engrossed—emphasis on the *grossed*.

The lovesick hugging and cooing seemed to go on for hours—torturous, endless, *please let the horror end* hours. Finally, they broke apart and Wade wrapped an arm around

Avalon. They turned and walked across the grass without looking back, not even acknowledging that Halley had seen the whole thing.

Halley felt a deep, searing ache shoot through her torso. Had she pulled a muscle? Or was this some sort of phantom pain, like an imaginary knife being stabbed repeatedly into her back? Her face contorted in misery. Silent tears streamed down her face and everything went cold. She felt mortified, devastated, and had the distinct sensation that she was about to pass out.

"Hey, what's up?" Kimberleigh bounded up behind Halley. Everything went black.

"Halley? Halley. Halley!"

She wanted to open her eyes, but her head was pounding and the light above her was too intense. She could feel soft blades of grass tickling her arms and legs as she lay stiff and uncomfortable. Where was she? How had she gotten here? And who kept screeching her name?

Finally, slowly, her pale blue eyes began to open. That was when she saw the person leaning over her: Avalon, her expression all wide-eyed, innocent concern. There were other figures around her, but Halley's eyes zoomed in on just one: Wade.

Halley tried to lift and shake her head as the memory of what had just happened came flooding back. She dug deep inside herself, channeling every ounce of strength she had.

She clenched her fists, reached up, and pushed Avalon out of the way. Halley rose to her feet—a little shaky at first, but then solid.

"Are you okay?" Sofee asked, running up to grab Halley's hand. She looked guilt-ridden—as if *she'd* done anything wrong. "I'm so sorry. I was on the phone when you fell. I got here as fast as I could!"

"Yeah, kiddo . . . does anything feel broken?" Fear flickered across Abigail Brandon's face as she reached out to take her daughter's other hand.

"Can you walk?" Charles asked, placing a strong, fatherly hand on Halley's shoulder.

"Yup . . . I think so. I'm fine." Halley nodded as she smiled at Sofee, her parents, Tyler, and Kimberleigh—all the people who really cared, who really loved her. "In fact, I'm better than fine. Barbecue of champions, anyone?"

"Well played," Sofee whispered in Halley's ear as she squeezed her hand.

Halley smiled confidently and marched off the grass with throngs of supporters beaming all around her. With each step she took, she felt stronger. And when she shot one final glance back at Avalon and Wade, Halley had every reason to believe things would work out just fine. After all, she'd proven herself a winner. And if there was one thing winners knew, it was that you can never give up on what you truly want. Not without a fight, anyway.

Is Halvalon over for good?
Find out in

GLAMNESIA

a Frenemies novel by Alexa Young

Acknowledgments

I've learned so much about friendship—and what that crazy concept really means—since I began writing this series. For me, it's all about love, support, and a bold yet benevolent brand of honesty. With that, I must first extend my sincerest gratitude to the readers and reviewers; your passion for books keeps authors like me doing what we love to do. I'm also beyond thankful to the cool chicks at Alloy Entertainment (that includes you, Josh) and HarperTeen, and to Jodi Reamer; I could not ask for better cheerleaders and reality-checkers than all y'all.

Then there are the incredible people I've been fortunate enough to call friends—some for a lifetime. I'm actually a shockingly popular person (or at least I have been on occasion), so this is in no way the exhaustive list:* Kristen Anderson, Sena Baligh, Jennifer Banash, Carolyn Brann, Katie

Cartwright, Tera Lynn Childs, Wendy Converse, Nancy Gottesman, Bethany Gumper and all the old *Shape*sters, Julie Jacobs, Lisa Jenkins, Brynja Kohler, Stephanie Kuehnert, Karen Lamberton, Bobby Lavelle, Carolyn Mackler, Annissa Mason, Allison Meyerson, Keri Mikulski, Taylor Morris and the good old *Jump* staff, Darren Murtari, Melissa O'Brien, Irene O'Connell, Sura Radcliffe, Emily Renninger, Erika Schultz, Michele Simon, Rebecca Slavin, Nicole Tocantins and all the *Hits* losers, Julie Wagner, Melissa Walker, the West Valley Moms and West Valley Players (yes, Sheri Kirby, especially *you*), Kerri Wolff, Rebecca Woolf, and finally, Lindsay Zimmermann (you may be last on this list, but you were my first BFF!).

Whew! And *finally*, to my family* for their unrelenting enthusiasm, encouragement, and all the other awesome-relative stuff: Thank you, Mom and Dad, Jon and Maggie, Zach and Nate, Chris and Raroo, Dene and Rich, Ken and Marge, and—my heart, my soul, the people who make every day an adventure (usually in the best possible way)—Joel, Jack, and Sydney (dogs are people too).

XOXOXO

* *To send hate mail and/or request an acknowledgment in book three, please contact me via my website: www.alexayoung.com.* ☺

ALEXA YOUNG lives in the Los Angeles area her husband and son.

Fi

The

Ho

For

best